Cattails for Sophie

Cattails for Sophie

Victoria Hand

Rutledge Books, Inc. Danbury, CT

Copyright © 2000 by Victoria Hand

ALL RIGHTS RESERVED
Rutledge Books, Inc.
107 Mill Plain Road, Danbury, CT 06811
1-800-278-8533
www.rutledgebooks.com

Manufactured in the United States of America

Cataloging in Publication Data
Hand, Victoria
   Cattails for Sophie

   ISBN: 1-58244-067-0

   1. Fiction. 2. Friendship. 3. Coming of Age.

Library of Congress Card Number: 00-100844

This book is dedicated to the love of my life Tim Grossi; my best friends, Sue Kent, David Wyatt, Jr. and Felice Wyatt, and my strength, my mother, Eva Wyatt and my late father, David Wyatt Sr.

Foreword

You have to understand, I'm here because of a combination of the good and bad things in life. When I look back, I probably wouldn't change anything. You have to realize that everything is not just black and white. People don't just do something because of one specific thing. It's a combination of things. Other people created my morals and character. I sure as hell wasn't born this way. Forget that garbage and just let me explain who those people were and what part they played. I am not going to tell you every little detail, just the important stuff. Let me get started, because this is going to take a little time.

One

I was on the back porch of our apartment on Dorchester, located on the south side of Chicago at 67th Street. This was an old, gray frame building with clothes hanging from everyone's balcony. The tenants were colored and white. It really didn't matter, because everyone lived from payday to pay day.

Our neighbors that lived below us were the Smiths. I ran downstairs and knocked on the door. Mrs. Smith opened it and smiled, "Tori, I know you are looking for Johnny, he is just washing up. Do you want to come in and have some pound cake while you wait"? "No thank you, Mrs. Smith. I'll just wait by the stairs for Johnny." I liked Mrs. Smith. She always had a smile on her face and her house smelled like vanilla or cinnamon. She was always picture perfect in a dress with an apron, almost like out of some magazine or something. Her aprons were stiff and white, and tied with a big bow in the back. I bet it took her an hour just to iron that apron.

Johnny was the same age as me: four almost five. He was also colored. He had brown hair like little, fine wire circles. His eyes were brown and lit up like a light bulb. His skin was soft and smelled of Vaseline. I was sitting on the steps when out he ran, grabbing my arm as he dragged me out to play. "Come on Tori, let's play catch!" "OK, Johnny. Wait for me." I ran to keep up with him.

We threw a ball back and forth, jumping up and down. It was early afternoon. We hung over the edge of the banister looking down into the alley, trying to figure out what to do next. Johnny hollered, "Tori! Let's run down the stairs and see who can get back to the top first." I knew Johnny would. First of all because he had more strength than me. Second, because I would let him. He did not like being beaten by me at anything. Because I loved him so much, it did not matter whether I won or not. I had not yet learned to compete or that winning was a necessity.

Johnny came lugging a great big, cardboard box, that once had a refrigerator in it. "Tori, look what I found!"

"Holy cow, where did you get that?" I questioned.

"My mom just got a new refrigerator. This will make a great tent. We can set it up in the yard!" he said with excitement.

"Here let me help." I said as I grabbed the back of it. We dragged it into the back yard and set it on its side. Then we both crawled in and laid down. It was perfect. We could actually sleep in it.

He killed me. He really killed me. It was perfect. Now we had to convince our mothers to let us spend the night in it. I went in the house and grabbed a blanket and my pillow. As I started dragging them down the stairs, Mother got a gander at me. "Tori! What are you doing with that blanket and pillow?"

"I am taking them out to our tent in the back yard," I said while continuing down the stairs.

"No you're not! You get back in here. It is getting dark outside." Mom said rather sternly.

"Please Mom, pretty please. Just this once. We are leaving tomorrow. Can't I just spend my last night in our tent that Johnny found?" I begged.

"No Tori! You cannot stay outside. You'll catch a cold. Maybe you can set the tent up in here in the living room," she said pointing to an open spot. Part of the furniture was already gone. It was then that it dawned on me that we were really leaving this place. I just started crying and couldn't stop.

"I'll tell you what. I will let you and Johnny stay out in the tent until ten o'clock. Then you have to come in the house. How about that?"

"I love you Mom. I can't wait to tell Johnny." I said as I ran off.

Mother made fried pies and she came outside with them for us to eat. Johnny loved Mother's fried pies. This time we got the apricot ones; my favorite. We sat on the steps and crammed them in our mouths as if we had been starved for days. Johnny ate two and I ate one. These fried pies were big, shaped like half moons. The edges were pronged with a fork to cover up the filling inside. They were crispy on the outside from being fried in lard. The dough was the same as biscuit dough. Mother must have made the pies because she felt sorry that we had to say good-bye to each other. Johnny didn't cry, but I sure did.

 This is the earliest part of my life that I can remember.

Two

I had not yet turned six. It was summer and my birthday didn't come until November. I got into the car and sat in the back seat. A woman with long blond hair and bright red lipstick opened the front door and was crying. I said, "Can we help you?"

She said, "No!"

My father came running up and yelled "Get the hell out of here!" At first I thought Dad was being horrible. Then it dawned on me that she was his girlfriend.

Joe and Kate got in the car and we all sat quietly as we headed toward the movies. Joe was my older brother and Kate, my older sister. They could pass as twins with their bright red hair and freckles galore. They rolled over what just happened. They did this probably for my benefit. I just couldn't let it slide. I started worrying. I worried about that woman. I worried about my mother. I worried about Kate and Joe. This was probably the day I became known as a worrywart.

That night when we got home, I was sick with a terrible sore throat. Grandma Rosie was worried about me. She set me on her knee and bumped me up and down, singing, "Shoe fly Shoe; Tori my Do Do, Shoe fly Shoe; I love you!"

I giggled, "Come on Grandma, do it again."

"Come on Tori, let me get this done." She then heated a long towel and filled it with hot cornmeal and muster role, and neatly pinned it around my neck. "Now tomorrow morning that nasty sore throat will be gone," she promised.

She carried me to bed and laid me sideways so that Joe and Kate could fit in with me. We lived in a two bedroom, brick bungalow on Van Vlissingen Street in Chicago. The area was known as Jeffrey Manor. Grandma had a twin bed in the same room with us, and Mom and Dad had their own room.

When I got up the next day, Grandma was right as usual, my throat was fine, so I got to go to the show. The movie house was on Commercial Avenue, a couple of blocks from our house. It was a brick building that had little folding chairs inside it. Frankenstein was showing. I was so terrified about him getting loose, I almost wet my pants. I just stuck my fingers in my ears and shut my eyes for the rest of the movie. I wasn't a movie buff, but I sure liked the penny candy.

Kate, Joe, and my cousin, Rose, were walking down the street with me from the movie house. Suddenly, Joe hollered: "Duck!" A big rock hit me in the head. Blood squirted all over my face and we all started running toward our house.

As we entered the house, Kate started yelling, "That Catholic boy that lives down the street hit Tori with a rock!"

Dad started screaming, "I have had it with those Catholics. I know that little bastard. I am going to go talk to his parents." Out the door he went. I sat there as Grandma cleaned up my face and made me lie down so she could put pressure on my wound.

Dad came storming back in the house and told everyone about how he told those Catholics off. I wondered if Catholics were some kind of monsters from another planet. I was a nothing, not a Catholic, Baptist, or Jew. I guess you could assume our family to be Southern Baptist. I was never required to attend church. I can't recall my parents ever attending a church of any kind either. Of course Dad always went around quoting the Bible and he sang hymns a lot. "Washed in the Blood of the Lamb," or something like that, was a favorite of his.

Annie Weiss was my new best friend and her brother, Bobbie was Joe's best friend. They lived next door to us. They were Jewish, but I didn't care. I really thought they were great, even though Dad thought the same of them as he did the Catholics. I thought, I would die for Annie. Annie was a little adult that I could relate to. We had a field in our back yard with tall grass and wheat and big brown cattails. Annie and I would spend our days running in the fields and discovering all the beautiful wild flowers, honeysuckles, sunflowers and such.

Joe had another friend, Clarence. He was much older than Joe. I would say about twelve. Annie and I hated Clarence. We got chills all over every time he came around. Joe and Clarence were playing ball in the back yard when Annie and I walked past them. Clarence stood still and eyed us up and down, and got a smirk on his face. He was a lot bigger than Joe, with black hair and jagged teeth.

"Tori, I don't like him. He is creepy," Annie said as we walked into her house.

"I know. Every time we walk by him I get the creeps. I don't know why, but I get the hebbie gebbies."

"Me too! I wonder why?" She said inquisitively.

"I don't know. I just want to stay as far away from him as I can. I can't believe Joe hangs around him," I responded.

"I think Joe feels sorry for him. Besides, he doesn't look at Joe like he looks at us. Come on let's go get our bird books and see if we can find that red bird we saw yesterday."

"Yes, wasn't she beautiful? I would love to catch her and keep her."

"Tori, you're crazy. We can't catch that bird. She is too fast for us."

We scampered off to the living room, hunting the bird book down, forgetting Clarence.

The next morning I was in the field by myself, picking cattails. Clarence just popped up out of the tall grass. I started running for home. The house looked about a mile away. However, it was a hop, skip and jump. As I sprung, so did Clarence after me. The next thing I realized, I was at the house in the bathtub. This was when I started taking two baths a day if I could get away with it. Mother seemed so proud of me. I was now a five year old that loved to take her own baths, at least two a day, alone, and wash the hell out of her hair.

A few months went by and Grandma sat me down to tell me she was leaving. She wanted to go and see her other kids. I asked when she was coming back and she said she wasn't sure. As Dad loaded everything in her car, we were all crying like it was the end of the world. I had a gnawing feeling in the pit of my stomach wondering if I would ever again see this great statue of a woman. She picked me up and swung me around saying, "I love you my Tori, My Do Do."

    Dad idolized Grandma. Since he was the baby in the family he was a mama's boy. I was a daddy's girl, probably because I was the baby and looked like my father. Dad was thin with blue eyes and a reddish-blond receding hairline. One might describe him as a Bing Crosby. He could even sing like Bing. Dad was more upset than everyone realized. I could see it in his face. He was going to miss his wonderful mother.

Three

It was a beautiful May day. I sat on my Aunt Dora's swing looking at the magnolia trees, thinking the flowers looked like birds. Everyone was whispering around the house and Dad finally arrived. He sat everyone down at Aunt Dora's table and announced he would be leaving for West Virginia. He said Grandma Rosie was not well and that he was going to see her. I screamed, "I want to go too!" He said, "No!" and hurried out of the room.

All my cousins seemed to act as if nothing was wrong. They were laughing and playing while Aunt Dora sat and talked about herself. Mom was very quiet and seemed to be worried. As upset as Mom was, she tried to get everyone together to go home and pack Dad's things.

Mother was a little tiny person with brownish-red hair and glasses. Joe and Kate got all their red hair and freckles from her. She was always reading something. Every time anyone wanted to know something, Mother was the one to ask. She worked hard every day as a waitress. That was why we had someone with us in the early years. My mother was the complete opposite of my father. She was not too friendly. She never ran up to us kids and hugged and kissed on us, nor did she want us to do the same to her. She was strong in her beliefs of being responsible for one's actions and taking care of family. She is where I received my sense of drive.

The next day, I was in the house with my cousins, Mary and Tommy. I could hear Mom crying. We all ran into the room and she announced that Grandma had died. My heart started pounding and I shook all over. I ran outside to the swing set and screamed and cried at the top of my lungs. I looked up to the sky and screamed, "God, oh God, why Grandma? Who are you or what are you to do such a thing to my Grandma? God, tell me they are lying. God, just bring her back so I can say good-bye." I cried for three hours until it was dark.

While I was in a state of grief, my cousin's were throwing Grandma's clothes and shoes in the yard and playing dress up with them. I had to control myself from grabbing the nearest blunt object and knocking them dead in their tracks. I hated them. They seemed like robots with no feelings at all.

In July, we moved into our new home located in a burb of Chicago called Sauk Village. As we drove down the dirt street, all of us kids sat, in the back seat somber faced about leaving our cousins and friends behind. It was like entering another world. The drive seemed to last for hours, but it was only twenty-five minutes from our old house. The house was a ranch with a basement. It was white with a bay window and a front and back concrete stoop, one of the larger homes on the block. As I scanned it, I became impressed. It sure was a lot bigger than our old house, and brand spanking new.

We all piled into the house lugging our prized possessions, claiming our piece of territory. Kate and I got one bedroom, Joe his own private haven, and naturally Mom and Dad had theirs. Our new home was like a palace compared to the house in Chicago. I thought we had become rich overnight. Kate really was upset about sharing a room with me. I felt bad for her. She was always the good little person in the family. She had a faith in God that I envied. She never used foul language, and always presented herself with class. Kate was also beautiful.

Joe, on the other hand was different. He had no religious convictions and used the word "fuck" in every sentence. He was like me in so many ways, especially his dark side. What I considered to be a dark side was the side of discontentment with life or a sadness that existed from an awareness of too much. The only quality that Joe had that I didn't, was talent. He could play a guitar or accordion by ear and sing. That really annoyed me.

The roads were sand and there were only about eight little houses on our block. Joe and I played games of hide-and-seek and loved crawling down in empty foundations, to hide. Across the street, a creek ran through the village where a lot of muskrats, rats, and mice lived. All these little creatures had not yet been ran out of town because the community was just being developed. Honeysuckles grew up on the embankments along with large sunflowers, and cattails. This summer we all enjoyed setting up our new home and exploring the surrounding areas.

Then came school. I dreaded going to school. As I walked down our street heading for a model home that was used for a school, I tried to figure out how to vomit, cut my leg, or bloody my nose to keep from having to continue on. Surely, Mom would let me stay home if something drastic happened. I pondered and squirmed all the way to the door and then I was there. My first year in school had been no where near as traumatic, because I knew the other kids.

As I walked in, there was a brown-haired, brown-eyed, elderly woman called Mrs. Fockler. She had a sweet little smile on her face and greeted everyone in the same manner. As I sat at my desk I could feel my face burning with fear. Now this fear was not a fear of my peers, but a fear that Mrs. Fockler knew more than me. Probably this was the insane part of my personality. As the day went by, I just stayed in my corner and kept my mouth shut. I learned that if I said nothing, then no one could realize just how dumb I was. I kept this philosophy throughout life. I did learn to relate to Mrs. Fockler though. She became the only person I felt at ease with. In my later years I came to realize what a great teacher she was.

Four

Mother sat me down to talk to me about having to go to the hospital.

"Tori, I have to go into the hospital in a few days."

"Why Mom?"

"Well, I am not feeling well and the doctors want to keep an eye on me."

"Are you going to be OK?" I was now worrying.

"Yes, I am going to be fine. When I come home you will have a new brother or sister."

I already knew a baby was coming. I just didn't know it was this soon. "Great Mom, I can't wait," I lied. All, I could think of was who was going to take care of this baby. Mom had to get back to work.

Dad came running into the house, "Hey, where is everyone? Come here. I have an announcement to make." Joe, Kate and I, lined up in the kitchen. "You have a new baby sister!" Dad boasted.

"Great Dad! How is Mom?" Kate asked.

"Your mother is fine."

"When are they coming home?" I inquired.

"The day after tomorrow."

I was relieved that Mom was OK and the baby was a girl. I sure didn't want to have to change a boy's diapers.

Now I had a new responsibility, a little red-headed baby sister that couldn't tell me what she wanted, but just wailed to the top of her lungs all the time. Every time I looked at her, I was amazed at how much hair she had. Two days old and more hair than I had at ten. Is that fair? Her little mouth was perfect and she had the biggest dimples you could imagine. My parents decided to call her Anastasia, sometimes known as Stacie. I thought, well that is better than Toria Cornelia Kilarney. Who in God's name ever came up with the name Cornelia? I thought about this quite a bit. Who the hell would want to be called Cornelia? I swore that I would never hang my kid with any name they would be embarrassed with.

While trying to fold the sheets, an older balding fellow came up to me and asked, "Are you here by yourself?"

I said, "Yes."

He asked where my parents were and I told him at home. I stood there hoping he was going to take me away from it all. He started showing me how to fold the sheets. He then asked how old I was. I said "ten." His eyes rolled around in apparent exasperation. I thought, Christ, here is another one looking down on me, feeling sorry for this poor little blue-eyed strawberry blond, with great big white teeth and the frail figure of a little girl. I told him that I could fold my own sheets and thanked him for his kindness. Then my mind starting running wild. I would have liked to kill that bastard. I hate it when people feel sorry for me. Damn it.

I was already infuriated over having to do the laundry at the laundromat, much less having all the adults looking at me with pity. As I folded the baby clothes, I began to realize just how much I hated being the responsible one.

Sauk Village was a poor community of blue collar workers trying to make their house payments. It was not the Heights or any move up like I had earlier believed. Dad was now a real drinker and gambler.

Since Grandma died he just went to shit. Mom was commuting to the loop every day going to work as a waitress trying to keep a house over our heads and her marriage together. It seemed there was never a happy day in our house during this time. Mother would come home from work exhausted, run to her bedroom close the door, escape into her books, and go to sleep. Dad, on the other hand, was out drinking or gambling away all the money he made by leasing gas stations.

One night, for some reason, I was left at home alone with Stacie. A lady was stabbed eleven times the night before and it was all over the news. I ran to the kitchen and got a butcher knife and sat near Stacie, wondering if the murderer was coming to get me. As I sat there shivering, I decided the element of surprise was best. So I covered the knife and slid my hand under the covers hanging on to the handle, waiting just waiting. To my relief, an hour later Mother made it home and rescued me. This was probably the most exciting thing that happened to me other than a woman neighbor molesting me when I was nine. I knew better, even though I was nine. So why didn't I tell anyone or go screaming out of her house? I later decided I was a pervert. This was a time that I learned most people have a perverted side. The smart ones learn to control their perversions or not act them out.

Five

Sophie Eaton was beautiful even at the age of ten. She had big white teeth, perfect skin, raven hair and brown eyes with a perfect shape. Sophie and I became best friends as soon as we met. We were both ten years old. One day, we hiked to Plum Creek. It was about five miles from my house. We picnicked on the creek bank. The bank had cattails growing along the edges with wild flowers melting into the prairie. The day was perfect, nothing but blue skies. Sophie and I crawled around looking for anything alive and to our surprise found a box nosed turtle. Sophie spotted it first. "Hey Tori, look here. It's a funny looking turtle. Look at how cute he is."

"Shit Sophie, it is ugly."

We couldn't believe it, a box on the end of a turtle's nose. We couldn't wait to get home to tell our parents about that funny looking turtle.

First we got to Sophie's house. "Mom, hey Mom, you're not going to believe what we saw at Plum Creek."

"What did you see?" Mrs. Eaton was saying as she walked in.

"A turtle that had a box on its nose."

"Are you sure? I have never seen a turtle with a box at the end of it's nose."

"Yes Mom, I am sure. Ask Tori." Mrs. Eaton turned toward me with a raised eyebrow.

"I swear, Mrs. Eaton. It had a box on the end of it's nose."

"Well, you two might have discovered something that no one else has ever seen," Mrs. Eaton said. Sophie just beamed at such an idea. She grabbed my arm and started dragging me toward my house so we could tell my mother about our discovery. My mother wasn't nearly as interested as Sophie's, she just pretended to listen while she cooked dinner while fading off into some state.

Sophie and I spent a lot of time in her back yard. She always dreamed about the future and carried me along. "Tori, when you grow up, what do you want to look like?"

"Well, I guess I would like to have big tits and be beautiful. How about you?"

"Who wouldn't want big tits? I'll settle for medium size ones."

The next thing we heard her mother giggling. We both turned beet red and ran to the far corner of the yard, so her mother couldn't hear anymore of our dreams. I thought it was downright rude for her mother to hang near the window and eaves drop on us. "Damn it, Sophie, I bet she would have a fit if we did that to her."

"Now Tori, you know it was innocent. Besides, she is my mother."

A few weeks later Sophie and I found a dead robin in my

back yard. We cried and had a funeral for it. Before the eulogy, we thought we should stuff the bird. I went and got a knife and some toilet paper.

"Tori, you're the brave one, you cut him and stuff him."

"No way, not me, you do it."

"Come on Tori, I know you can do it, I just can't." I picked up the knife and put the point on the bird's breast. I just couldn't do it. I lost my nerve. What a damn chicken shit. I was really upset that I didn't have the nerve.

"Sophie, I just can't do it. I don't want to see its guts pour out of her."

"Aw, come on Tori ... please?"

"OK, but you're going to have to help." I laid the bird on its back with its feet straight up in the air. Its beak was yellow and it looked like its tongue was hanging out, or something was. I took the knife from the point and poked it into its chest. I don't know what I hit, but some brown stuff oozed out. That was when Sophie started puking.

"Stop it! Stop right now. How awful. Poor bird." She cried in between heaves.

"Damn it Sophie. You wanted me to do this."

"I don't care. It is terrible. Lets just bury the poor bird."

I immediately stopped, relieved that I didn't have to go any further. What a mess.

We found an empty shoe box in my house. "Let's put toilet paper in the bottom to make a little bed," I said. Sophie ran and got the toilet paper. We must have put a whole roll in the box. I picked up the poor little bird with toilet paper and rolled her up. Sophie put the top on the box and we both started bawling. We went outside behind our garage and dug a little hole. By that time we were hysterical. I was appointed by Sophie to do the committal. I said,

"Dear God, please make sure that this little bird makes it to heaven with you. Thank you Lord, Amen."

"Amen," Sophie squeaked between the tears. God, what would I do if something ever happened to Sophie, I thought.

Joe was playing with Jeff, Sophie's Brother and I could not help being intrigued with what they were doing. Taking baby mice and throwing them up in the air and watching them splatter when they hit the ground. This little lesson taught me that girls are really different from boys, no matter what anyone says. My heart started throbbing as I looked at the little gray pelts lying smashed on the sidewalk. I worried for a long time whether Joe was going to be a mass murderer. Sophie just cried and cried each time one hit the ground.

We decided to go horseback riding with my brother and Sophie's brother Jeff. Sophie was a nervous wreck, crying and saying she couldn't get on the horse. Finally, after we got her on the horse, she started screaming. As I looked around, the horse took off like a bolt of lightning down the trail with Sophie holding on for dear life. We all chased after her and finally caught up with her, calmed her and her horse down. She was crying and choking saying, "Look at my leg. That damn horse bit me. I didn't do anything to that damn horse and it bit me." Poor Sophie, her entire thigh was black and blue. She swore that she would never get on a horse again.

Cattails for Sophie

"Aw, come on, Sophie quit being such a baby. Get back on it," I begged.

"Hell no," she hollered as she started back to the stables. The more that I thought about it the more I agreed with her. Her leg could have been bitten right off.

We were back in school and my birthday was November 2nd and Sophie's was December 2nd. That year I got two turtles for my birthday. They came with a little bowl that had a palm tree on an island, for the turtles to climb. I called Sophie all excited, "Hey, Sophie, guess what I got for my birthday."

"Aw, come on, Tori, I don't know, just tell me."

"Two turtles with a bowl with an island in the middle of it," I gloated.

"I'm on my way!" she croaked. She was huffing and puffing as she scrambled in the door.

"They are so cute," she blurted out between gasps for air. "Come on, let's take them outside and put them in the grass," I said as I grabbed my new found friends. Sophie and I considered these turtles as all of our other little creatures our new found friends. We proceeded out the door, down the stairs and out to the back yard.

"What do you think I should call them?"

"How about Bibbie and Bobbie?", she mumbled as she grabbed them and set them on the grass.

"No, what about Ishcabibble and Ishcabobble?"

"Yes, Tori, that's it. Ishcabibble and Ishcabobble. I nudged their rear ends trying to get them to run, but they stayed dead in their tracks. Sophie started rambling about something or another, and I swear I only looked at her for a second, next thing you know the turtles were gone. I thought the end of the world had come. It was cold outside and I knew if we didn't find the turtles they would die.

"Damn it, Sophie, they are going to die," I cried. She was crying so hard I thought she was going to have a heart attack. I guess I was crying just as hard. We crawled all over the back yard for at least two hours, but to our dismay, no Ishcabibble or Ishcabobble.

Next came Sophie's birthday. She got two hamsters. They were the greatest things since the chameleons we could pin to our collars. They were furry and lovable, clean and could run very fast. Their cage smelled like cedar and they even ran around on a little wheel.

I was sitting in the kitchen with Dad and Sophie came running in the house crying and screaming hysterically, "He's dead, he's dead. It was terrible!" Dad got so upset he didn't know what to do. She kept mumbling something and Dad thought that he heard her father died. He hugged her and tried to calm her down but she was out of control.

I was trying to understand what had happened. Finally, through the tears and mumbling, I realized that Puff had died. I started screaming and crying hysterically and Dad was about to run down the street, until he heard me say, "Puff?" "Who the hell is Puff?" Dad said. I explained it was one of the hamsters. Dad lost all his sympathy and was ready to kill Sophie and me.

"Oh Tori, it was terrible, Puff suffered so much. I think she choked to death. Promise me, you'll never let me suffer if I get sick. Please promise me!"

"Shit, Sophie, you ain't going to get sick."

"Promise!" she cried. "I promise damn it, I promise."

We had another funeral. Sophie made this cute little coffin out of one of her jewelry boxes. Puff was lying there enveloped in toilet paper, looking like she was sleeping.

"Tori, you have to say something."

"Dear Lord, please take care of Puff and thank you Lord for taking him to Heaven and not letting him get smashed like those little mice our brothers killed." Sophie closed the lid and put Puff in the hole next to our dead bird. I pushed the dirt on top of him.

"Tori, don't forget your promise."

"I won't, Sophie. You have to promise me too."

"I promise," she said.

Six

We made it through eight years of school and were graduating. Sophie was thrilled with the idea of going to high school. We would curl each other's hair and try on all our dresses to see what looked the best for graduation. "Tori, what do you think you will be when you get out of school?"

"I hope a history maker, but probably some damn drunk like my Father."

She frowned and then said, "If anyone can make history, it's you. You'll never be a drunk."

"Shit, Sophie I love you!"

I really admired her so much. She always made me feel good. Not matter what happened she was always positive and loving. A lover would best describe her, a real lover.

I wanted a new dress like all the rest of my peers, along with flowers, pictures, a party and gifts. What a spoiled little brat, expecting all of those things. I approached mother when she came in, and she said that she could not afford a dress that I would have to wear Kate's graduation dress, which was only four years old. I was devastated. I cried and carried on like a little demon, never realizing just how much I was hurting my mother. Dad was worse than ever, staying out all night and coming home drunker than a skunk. He would usually threaten Kate or Mother. Well graduation came, I wore the old dress and Dad barely made the ceremony. My poor mother somehow got me flowers and had a cake. She also wrote me a note:

"Dear Tori,

I am so sorry that I could not afford to buy you a new dress for Graduation. I realize how much it means to you and hope that you understand that it is not because I don't love you. Please try to understand and forgive me.

Love,
Mother

Mother had the innate sense of making me feel like shit. Somehow, I seemed frustrated that I could not let her know how much I was really aware of her situation with Dad and his gambling. I always felt that I was better off silent than embarrassing her or degrading her in any way, by making her aware of my knowledge. Still, I desired the things that my peers had and a home life similar to theirs. A father that didn't drink and a mother that was home cleaning house and taking care of us kids.

Sophie was in the same shape I was. No way could her parents afford a new dress for graduation. So we both sulked for a while and then forgot about it. I was the one that sulked the most. Sophie was too considerate. For some reason she could let things go easier than me.

Aunt Suzanne blew into town one afternoon with a new husband. She grabbed me up and kissed me. Then she screeched, "Look at you Tori. You are so beautiful!"

I mumbled back, "So are you!"

Aunt Suzanne would babysit for Mother every chance she got while in town. She was always telling everyone how much she loved them and was full of compliments. She was really a bubbly type of person, except when she was down. It was like a roller coaster.

I loved seeing Aunt Suzanne because she reminded me of Grandma Rosie. Both were such loving people. The only difference was Grandma Rosie was never on a downer. Grandma Rosie was not even her mother. They just reminded me of each other. Aunt Suzanne would get up and make us scrambled eggs with cole slaw and toast. Sounds icky, but it was great. Then she would turn on the radio to some country western station and start singing out loud. Then out came the Jack Daniels and she would start saying, "I sure would like to blow my damn brains out."

I would say, "No you wouldn't, cause you would never see me again." She would then perk back up, smile a big smile and pass out. Then she blew out of town, as fast as she blew in. I worried about my Aunt Suzanne. Why couldn't she be happy?

Sophie was around me all the time, even when company came. "Tori, do you think your Aunt is nuts?"

"No way, why do you think she is?"

"Well, anyone that is always threatening to kill themselves must be a little whacked."

"No, Sophie, you don't have to be nuts to want to be dead and out of misery. Aunt Suzanne just gets depressed sometimes like the rest of us. She's got more nerve than us. She just admits what most people are afraid to say. We all get down."

"No way do we get that down," Sophie shot back with a frown on her face. "And we all don't feel like blowing our damn brains out. I want to live life to its fullest!"

"You know Sophie, I don't want to ever die. I want to live forever, but shit happens. I just think that sometime or another everyone feels like blowing their damn brains out."

"Sophie, do you believe in God?"

"Geesus, Tori, how could you ask such a thing? Sure I believe in God!"

"Well, maybe I'm not asking the right question. Do you believe that we will rise again. You know, like they say in the Bible?"

"I don't know Tori, but I know I believe in God. Do you believe in God and rising from the dead?"

"I believe that God created us and he created every living thing. I don't believe that I am that important nor is any other mortal that important to be given eternal life like I would like to perceive eternal life to be."

"So, Tori, what you are saying is, when we are dead, we are dead and that is it."

"Yep, that is what I am saying. Dead is dead. We have one chance and we'd better make the best of it."

"You sure say that matter of factly. Almost like you know it to be the truth, the whole truth, and nothing but the truth. I don't want to close any doors. I would rather take my chances on there being something after death."

"Well, Sophie, just answer me this question. If there is life after death, then at what age will we be at when we come back to life?"

"I honestly believe that it will be the age that we were at our prime or our best or our happiest."

"What about the little babies that die? They didn't even get a chance for the best, or a little nine-year-old kid?"

"Tori, even if they had a breath of air in their bodies, that point might have been their best, or their prime and maybe they will get a chance to live longer in the hereafter."

"Are you saying that we will age in the hereafter?"

"Maybe, maybe not."

"Well, Sophie, that puts it all back to where we started from. Like say right now. If I died right now. I would want to come back as of right now and have you as my friend and my mom and dad as they are right now. Not when they were twenty years old or fifty years old. So I would probably be unhappy in the hereafter. Because I would want everything just like it is right now."

Seven

We were now in high school, Sophie and I. Still the best of friends, but we had let one more girl in our clique. Her name was Bernadette. Bern was the sister of my brother's friend Ron, whom I had a terrible crush on. She was tall and lanky, semi-average on looks but had a great personality, brown eyes and brown hair. Bern, Sophie and I were the three musketeers. Bloom High School had groups of kids that hung out together. There was the Foyer Gang, who consisted of snobs that thought they were better than everyone else, and then there were the low class, street kids. The three musketeers fell into that group.

Sophie and I were equal in intellect, so we could discuss our studies and world problems. Bern was just Bern. I was the leader of the pack. The three of us did not want to be plastic people, living in plastic houses, with plastic families, when we became adults. Plastic is a good synonym for cloned. We wanted to be different.

"Sophie what do you want to do with your life?" I questioned. "Maybe become another Madame Curie or Joan of Arc," she said with intensity.

"I want to become a history maker, not just a millionaire, a history maker. Maybe find a cure for cancer, or shape an ideal society. A society not like President Johnson's "Great Society," but an ideal society without welfare and drugs. A Society where we all work and provide for our families and have no addictions," I said.

"How could we obtain that type of life style?" Sophie questioned.

"I don't really know. If I did, I would be a history maker right now."

I had two major problems that I ran into while thinking about my ideal society. The first was instilling the ambition to work in all people. The second was to find a cure for addiction to drugs and booze. I figured if we could lick those two problems, we would have the ideal society.

It was the Summer of '65, we were going into our sophomore year. I was fourteen. I had blossomed into a big-busted, blue-eyed, strawberry blonde with great big, straight white teeth and full lips. Well I wished for big tits and I got them. Boys appeared to like me but never really approached me. We had a boy that lived next door that was rather handsome, but cocky. His name was Danny. Danny was blue-eyed, freckle- faced and medium built. He hung around older fellows with cars. He was always trying to tease me about something or another. One day he called me "chicken" because I wouldn't do it with him. He kept calling me "chicken" and did it in front of Bern and Sophie. Since I was the leader of the pack, it was impossible to let this slide. Being the leader of the pack meant being unafraid of anything.

I told him I was not a chicken and that I would meet him at 6:30 down the street and show him I was no chicken. Sophie, Bern and I went to the corner and he picked me up. We did the deed and he dropped me off. Sophie and Bern naturally wanted the details. I explained that I pulled down my pants and it felt like a big poker stuck me and it was as simple as that. I further explained that it was rather awkward, and not very exciting. All they had to do was watch a couple of dogs and they could get the picture. Nothing was romantic, sweet, or loving about this experience. Bern had a renewed respect for me.

Sophie was worried about me. Neither one of them would have just casually taken someone up on a dare to surrender their virginity. I figured that I was going to lose it someday, so what difference did it make that it was under these circumstances instead of for love. I didn't bleed like normal virgins. I wondered if it was because of that woman molesting me or some other reason.

Experiencing the unknown or forbidden is not all that it is cracked up to be. The anticipation is much more exhilarating than the deed. Sophie spent the night with me. She didn't bug me by being nosy. I hate nosy people. If I wanted to talk about it, Sophie knew that I would. Sophie respected people's privacy.

We were all living in times of the greatest sexual freedom, the greatest music and the best drugs or booze one could hope for. As summer turned into winter my interest in sex became pure lust when I fell in love with Ron. Ron was tall, with light brown hair, brown eyes and dimples. He was a little chubby with the cutest smile you ever saw in your life. We both had a mutual interest in each other. Our relationship was an experiment of lust, jealousy, torture and love. There was no intellectual side to it. There were never any discussions about politics, current events, history, or philosophy. He always teased me or winked and smiled at me, and I would just melt.

※

Our first escapade in the bedroom was in December. As Ron was swirling his tongue in my mouth he started to unbutton my blouse. I could feel the passion in my body start to rise from the bottom of my toes to the top of my head. As he laid me on the bed he started french kissing my ears, then my neck, and ran down to my breasts, licking, sucking, caressing. I thought, my God this is what everyone was raving about. He was tender and loving. Sparks of electricity were flying between us. I got a hot flash through out my body and then goose bumps all over. My heart was racing as I climaxed. Now I thought it was too bad I wasted my first time on a bet.

As we lay there holding each other, neither of us said anything. About an hour later I got up, dressed, and slipped out of the room. Then I started thinking, wondering if he felt the same about me. Was I good? What did he think of my body? Was I his girl? The next day he came running over to my house. We got in his car went and parked in the woods and started tearing off each other's clothes, again, never telling the other how we felt.

eight

Ron and I continued our love affair into the summer. Then, I had a party and invited over some friends. One of my acquaintances at that time was a rather homely-looking girl named Cecelia. She was thin with black hair and buck teeth. She came from a wealthy family. The minute she met Ron, she fell in love with him.

"Tori, he is gorgeous. Please introduce me to him." she begged.

I thought about it for a minute. I slowly walked toward him smiling a nervous smile. "Ron, you see that girl over there, her name is Cecelia, and she is nuts about you. She wants to go out with you. What do you say?" Never in a million years did I think he would go for it.

He smirked and said, "Well, Tori it is your call. Do you want me to meet her or not?"

I said, "Yes."

He said, "Are you sure?"

I said, "Yes." Hoping that he would say, "No way! I love you." He smirked at me and with a twinkle in his eye he said, "Sure I'll take her out".

That was it, I had now gambled away the love of my life. Wanting him to tell me first that he loved me, testing him, and playing a stupid little game. Naturally, they started seeing each other. No one could believe it. Everyone that hung out with us thought she was a dog. As time went by, she became obsessed with me. Night and day our phone would ring with hang ups. I could never figure this out. She had Ron, I had no one. I thought, "Why harass me?" I finally concluded she was insecure because of her homeliness. I made a vow to myself to never be that vulnerable.

Family life was more difficult day by day. Dad was now drunk every night and gambling all his money away. He was even to the point of holding guns to our heads. One evening he came home and started threatening Mother. Naturally, all of us kids stood there glaring at him, waiting for him to make a move. All of a sudden he went into the bedroom, grabbed a shotgun and waved it at each of us. Somehow, I slipped out of view, got to a phone, and called the Police. "Please come to 2224 210th Street, my father has a gun pointed at my mother," I screamed. Those creeps just came and calmed him down, leaving him there with the gun. We were all shaking as we eased into our rooms, hoping he would stay on the couch and sleep it off. I guess I shouldn't call the police "creeps." It wasn't their fault. The laws just sucked. Actually, they wanted to beat the shit out of Dad, but restrained themselves.

Nine

Joe was Conrad Birdie in the play "Bye, Bye, Birdie". He had on a gold suit and a speckled guitar hung over his shoulder as he walked out on stage. Sophie, Bern, Kate, Anastasia, Mother and I, all jumped up and started clapping. I could tell he was so embarrassed at our display of pride. All I could think of was how proud I was to be the sister of a soon-to-be movie star. He started singing "One Last Kiss". I just loved it when he shook his hips and imitated Elvis. We all started screeching. The year before, he was in the play "Oklahoma". This year he was cast in a perfect part. Joe sounded like a mixture of Elvis and Waylon Jennings. When the play was over, he would not even look our way. He just ignored us and went off with the rest of the cast for dinner. Funny thing how artists become so embarrassed by their work, especially when they perform for family or close friends. I guess it is OK to show your ass to strangers.

Sophie, Bern and I were now driving. Our evenings consisted of driving to the Dog n' Suds, sitting around and watching all the cars go by. Bern was growing farther apart from Sophie and me because of Ron. She always felt that I was her friend just because of her brother. Naturally, she had to pretend to like Cecelia, because things were getting serious. Ron would call me and try to get me to go out with him. I wouldn't consider it because he was still seeing Cecelia.

Sophie was dating a guy that lived across the street from her named Jim. He had freckles with brown hair and glasses, not the cutest guy in the world. Both were in "luv" with each other. You know, "Luv". Luv is a little love combined with a lot of lust. Bern was not dating anyone. I felt she was beautiful, but for some reason none of the boys liked her. It was the year of our Junior Prom and I had a job working at Discount Center as a waitress, cook and dishwasher. A real sweet guy that had a crush on me, asked me to the prom. Sophie had Jim, but Bern had no one to go with. Being a great leader, I begged my brother, Joe, "Please, oh pretty please, take her to the prom for me. I swear, I'll love you forever."

His response was, "Five dollars and a paper bag over her head."

This did not shake my confidence in him. "Aw, come on Joe. She has a great personality and she is cute. Please, just for me. Come on, please?"

"Damn it Tori, I will as long as she understands I am doing her a favor."

"No way, Joe. You're doing me the favor so she can't know about it."

"Damn it Tori, you are going to owe me big for this."

"I love you Joe, I really love you. I knew you would do this

Cattails for Sophie

for me, because you love me too." I smiled at him as he sulked.

I don't know why I agreed to go to the prom with James. I didn't really know him. He even had a mutual friend ask me. James was handsome and very reserved. He thought that I was gorgeous. Unfortunately, he had the most horrible time of his life. I was a bitch. I didn't even kiss him when we went to the Dunes. The Dunes was on Lake Michigan. It was the place that everyone went to mess around after the prom. Almost everyone stayed out all night. Naturally, Ron and Cecelia were there.

My evening was over after I got a gander at them necking. I was not interested in any man, because I still loved or lusted after Ron. I was never one to date for the sake of dating. Bern had become another story. She would sleep with anything. Sophie wanted to remain a virgin. Christ, that was really perfect. Sophie was always a virgin in my eyes, but that night was her night of deflowering. She did not talk about it except to mention the fact. I was gracious enough not to press her for details as a return favor from my experience. My brother was like me that night. He didn't even kiss Bern. I couldn't believe it. He could have gotten lucky, but he passed.

That summer, Bern got pregnant When I found out who the father was, I almost died. It was Ben, Cecelia's cousin. I knew that he was just doing her for the sake of getting a piece. Now what was she going to do? Illinois had outlawed abortions. Her parents would disown her, because they were Catholic. Somehow she got enough money together to go to New York. When she came back, our relationship changed.

Relationships never work out when you know all the skeletons in the other person's closet.

All through my high school years, my responsibilities consisted of taking care of Stacie, cooking and cleaning. One day after school I came home very sick. I started frying pork chops, and went to lie down. They started burning so I got up and grabbed the lid. The lid was hot as a firecracker, and fell out of my hand into the frying pan. The grease spewed all over, burning my face to the point of blisters. Now besides being sick, I was in pain from third degree burns. I still had to finish cooking, because Dad had called the house drunk out of his mind, letting me know to have his dinner ready.

When he sat down, he threw the pork chops across the table and screamed, "These are burned! I'm not eating this slop!".

My head was reeling, my face burning, so I lost control and said, "I don't give a shit." Then I started to head for my room to lie down.

Dad jumped up, grabbed me, and pinned me against the wall. He started choking and punching me. I was gasping for air, flailing around trying to get free, when Joe came in the house and screamed, "Dad, let her go!".

Joe was trying to pull Dad away, when all of a sudden Dad let go and looked at me with glassy eyes. I slumped down coughing, trying to catch my breath as the tears streamed down my face, running into my blisters, causing me even more pain.

As I got up, trying to compose myself, Dad said, "Here is twenty bucks, take the car and get yourself a hamburger."

Joe had run out of the house to get Ron for help. I grabbed the car keys, threw the money down, ran out of the house, jumped into the car, and started driving down the street. I was now hysterical. Joe was running along side of the car screaming, "Stop the car Tori!" I did. He jumped in and took me to Sophie's house. She took me in her room and put me in bed. The entire time she was crying . I don't know who I felt the sorriest for her, or me.

"I am going to kill that son of a bitch. I swear it. I am going to kill him!" Sophie raved. "How could he do this to you? What the fuck is wrong with him?"

"Geesus Sophie. He is a damn drunk. He didn't even know he did it after it was all over with."

"I don't care. He could have killed you."

When Sophie's mother got home she called my mother to come and get me. Mom got home from work at 6:00 P.M. When Mother looked at me, she turned white. I thought she was going to faint. My face was swollen and blistered, and my neck and chest were bruised from Dad beating and choking me. She got me in the car, took me home to confront Dad. He sat there and swore he never touched me. The only thing we could figure was that he blacked out. Well, this was the straw that broke the camel's back. Mother filed for divorce the next day. Nothing like being the one to break up a family. Instead of blaming Dad, I blamed myself for burning the pork chops. I should have ignored the burnt face and went on and cooked a new meal. The outcome would have been totally different.

Ten

We finally made our senior year in school. In grades one through eight I always got A's and B's. But in my junior year of high school, I just colored in boxes on the ACT by shutting my eyes and pointing to the answer without reading the question, or just dotting some kind of pattern. This year toward the end of school, I regretted my actions. I had always dreamed of being a doctor. Now I had nothing to look forward to. Sophie did better than me, she maintained a B average, but never really thought about going to college. Sophie had more control of herself. I could never understand how she had the discipline she had. Hell, her purse was even organized. I wanted to be more like her, but I had no control of myself.

Bern was becoming even more distant. Sophie was still dating Jim. I was now dating a young looking Paul McCartney, who was from Beckley, West Virginia, my birth place. His name was Jack. Jack was in love with me. He even went so far as to get me a ring. I was only seventeen when he got it. I accepted, praying that I would get out of this place. That song by the Animals was my motto. It went something like, "We got to get out of this place, if it's the last thing we ever do, girl there's a better life for me and you." I wasn't even sure of what would make me happy. I just knew that there had to be more to life than the little plastic town I was in.

Mother was devastated. "Tori, how could you? You're not even eighteen yet. Let me remind you that I am legally responsible for you until then and you are not going anywhere until you're of age."

"Mother, when I graduate, I am leaving home and there is nothing you can do about it!" I screamed running off into my room. That would be in five months. I was not in love with Jack. Ron was still in my heart. Jack was a southern gentleman. He opened car doors, never said shit, and always kissed me goodnight at the door. This was unusual. Most men had to be fought off.

Prom was coming and this year I wanted to look elegant. My hair was now a dark auburn, unless I spent time in the sun and then it was a strawberry blonde. I had Sophie put my hair up in banana curls. She loved to do hair. She wove a red ribbon through the curls. My shoes where red satin and I had a velvet red cape. My dress was a long white empire. When Jack came, he had a white tux on that made him even more handsome, with his black hair and deep brown eyes.

After pictures at my house, we picked up Sophie and Jim. Sophie was gorgeous. She wore a blue empire dress with long white gloves and her hair was puffed up in a bouffant hairdo. Jim had on a black tux with a blue cummerbund. They both looked absolutely perfect.

Our first stop was dinner at the Red Lion Restaurant. This was where everyone was going before the prom. We were eating dinner and I happened to look up at Sophie. I thought I was going to wet my pants. She had thousand island dressing all over her face, even up her nose and just kept on talking. I was laughing so hard, tears were streaming down my face, but I couldn't get the words out of my mouth. I kept motioning to my face and rolling my eyes. Finally, Jim leaned over and told her. She got up and ran to the bathroom. I was still laughing. When she came back to the table, I had calmed down, but she was super pissed. Now she wouldn't speak to me. She just leaned over and said, "Fuck you!" Christ, Sophie never swore. I worried about her staying mad at me, and of course, she did.

We went on to the Prom and then to the Dunes. Jack was now prepared to make his move. We started kissing and petting. I am now wondering why he wasn't hot. He whispers in my ear, "My dear, you are just lovely, but I need to tell you something. I have a heart condition that causes me difficulty in getting an erection." I thought, Christ, this is my fucking luck. I am going to marry a man that is impotent! I just whispered, "Don't worry darling, we can work things out." We then went swimming, played volleyball and ate our picnic lunch. Do I need to say more? Jack became history two weeks later. This was unfortunate for both of us. I loved Jack as a brother from the start. I was never in love with him. I honestly felt he had the same feelings for me.

I stayed at Sophie's house that night. When we got up in the morning she was humming some tune or another. "So, Sophie, how was your night?"

"Perfect, absolutely perfect! I loved every minute of it. I felt like a princess."

"You looked like a princess. You are a princess."

"Cut it out. You know what I mean. Everything was just perfect."

I just couldn't tell her about Jack. "Yes, it was perfect. Just peachy keen."

The big day finally arrived: Graduation Day. Sophie and I were at graduation, crying. We were the only two idiots crying. Everyone else seemed thrilled to be going on with their lives. Not us, we already knew how difficult life was, much less how much more difficult it was going to become. We reflected back on our high school years. The booze, sex and rock and roll were, great and horrible at the same time. How can that be? The Class of '69. We invented the symbol of "69" meaning oral sex. We didn't have a care in the world when it came to experimenting with every facet of sex imaginable, also, the music. Never in history will Rock and Roll be replaced with music more exhilarating. The goose bumps, the flush, rush and juices flow all at the same time.

"You know Sophie, this is it."

"What do you mean this is it?"

"Well, we have to get jobs and take care of ourselves."

"That is a given, Tori. We have known that for years."

"Yes, but now it is a reality. I never thought I would live to see this day."

"I didn't either. I guess everyone feels that way."

"If everyone felt that way, then why are we the only idiots crying?"

"I guess we are the only two that know the party is over."

We cried until our damn eyes were swollen, recognizing the sadness of the future, of the doom of adulthood.

Dad did not make the ceremony. He was now so bad with his drinking that he was considered a skid row bum. Mother got me a watch and had a little cake at the house for the immediate family. Sophie didn't even get a cake. I could not understand it. Her mom and dad were both working and together so there was no reason for them not even getting her a cake. I went to the store and got her a card then grabbed some cake and ran down to her house.

"Well, kid we made it." I said as I walked into her room.

She beamed, "I never thought we would. Now we have to get jobs. What are you going to do?"

"I'm going to stay waitressing until I find something better." I had a little part-time job waitressing at a local snack bar. Sophie had never worked.

"Well this will be my first job, so I guess I'll take what I can find, just for the experience," she said in between gulping down the cake.

Sophie got a factory job at J's Pizza with a guarantee of forty hours a week at minimum wage. She kept telling me how great it was until I finally relented into applying for a position. I was hired the next day. When I walked into the factory, everyone had nets on their heads and little white gowns with plastic gloves. It looked as if everyone was gearing up for surgery. I was given my garb to put on and then shown to my station. I was to stand around a bin where a retarded lady screamed to the line, "You who, you who, meat across the street! Meat across the street!" She would then throw frozen sausage that was in squares down into the bin for us to grab and break up and put on top of the pizzas. Sophie and I would grab the meat, break it up and throw it on the pizzas on a conveyor belt. It was like watching "I Love Lucy". After about four hours of this torture, I realized that Sophie had lost her mind. This job was for someone who had no mind. I went to the supervisor and gave her my condolences and left. Sophie just smiled and waved good-bye as I walked out the door.

A few weeks later I decided to go into downtown Chicago and try my luck. I applied for a job at Travelers Insurance and got it. I only stayed there for two weeks and discovered that insurance was not my game. I found a personnel service that had companies that paid the fees for the new employees. I made an appointment and went down for testing. The name of the company was #1 Personnel. When I went in, all the guys went "gaga" over me. They came up and asked me if I was a stewardess. At first I felt very special. But in came the next client and they treated her the same.

My consultant's name was Clay. Clay was from Iowa and cute as a button, but naive as hell. He told me that my test scores were excellent and he thought I might get a job at Bowes, Inc. They sold and manufactured office machines and copiers. I was further informed that Bowes, Inc. wanted people from the age of twenty-five and up that dressed conservatively and scored well on aptitude tests. The job started at $125.00 a week, which was about $50.00 higher than any place else. Clay scheduled an interview for 9:00 A.M. the following day.

When I arrived at Bowes, Inc., I was wearing a red dress with silver ruffled cuffs. As I walked through the place, everyone turned their heads and stared. Naturally, everyone there had little gray suits on. I now realized that I was in big trouble, because this dress was one of my most conservative ones. As I walked toward Mrs. Ryan's office I started getting cottonmouth and praying that I would land this job. She was vice-president in charge of sales. I walked into a modest office and came face to face with a tall, brunette with short hair, manicured finger nails with a Gray suit on. Her face was without expression, rather business like. She had a perfect mouth with dimples and a beauty mark similar to Liz Taylor's. When Mrs. Ryan looked at me, she tried to hide her disapproval of my dress code. After she finished interviewing me, I was taken into a room for an aptitude test. Upon completion of the aptitude test, I was taken back into her office. Then our conversation went something like this:

Mrs. Ryan:

Toria, your score on the aptitude test is one of our highest. We would be pleased to have you here as an employee of Bowes, Inc.. You can start on Monday.

Toria:

Thank you very much Mrs. Ryan. I appreciate the opportunity.

I was so excited. I ran back to #1 Personnel. Clay and the

staff couldn't believe that had I made it. I was the youngest person ever hired by Bowes, Inc.; seventeen and now entering the corporate structure. It was definitely better than making pizzas or working for an insurance company making $75.00 a week.

When I got home and told Mom and Kate, they were very happy for me. I then talked Kate into going to see Clay about getting her a job. Kate did get a job at World Life Insurance, so we got to commute downtown together.

Sophie was still working at the pizza factory. I kept trying to get her to go downtown with me to the personnel agency but she kept making excuses. Kate offered to try to get her into her firm. What a great sister. No other sister that I knew of would do that for her little sister except mine. "Oh Kate, you're the best. Please see what you can do. You just wouldn't believe what it is like making those damn pizzas." The next day, Kate had gotten Sophie an interview.

Sophie was immediately hired. "Tori, I got the job. I can't believe it! I got the job!"

"Aw Sophie, I am so proud of you. I knew you would get it. Now, tell me the truth, aren't you glad you don't have to make another pizza?"

"Yes siree Bob. Whoopee! I've got a new job! I've got a new job! I'm going to be a secretary! Whoopee!" she shouted as she danced around the room. Sophie tickled me to death. She was so excited about something I took for granted. "Tori, tell Kate that I love her and owe her for the rest of my life."

"I will, Sophie, I will."

It was my eighteenth birthday. The celebration was a week

Cattails for Sophie

long. First, Bern, Sophie and I got our stock of liquor. Bern: Schlitz Malt Liquor, Sophie: Apricot Brandy and Me: Peppermint Schnapps. We loaded up in the car and took off to a dance at Marvel Hall. On the way we drank our stash. We didn't just take a drink mind you, we guzzled our booze down in its entirety. By the time we hit the dance, we were bombed. Of course we partied even more until after 1:00 A.M. in the morning and then headed home. On the way home, I hung my head out the window vomiting all that day's nutrition, while Bern drove. It never ceased to amaze me how she and Sophie could hold their liquor. I must have heaved my guts out for at least a half hour. They dragged me in the house and threw me in bed. Thank God for friends. Sophie pulled my shoes off while Bern tucked me in.

The next night was an experience very difficult to acknowledge. Probably because I discovered, again, how exciting it is to be perverse. The evening started out by getting the same booze as the night before, and heading over to another girl's house that I casually knew named Birt. Now Birt was tall, blonde and built like a model, brilliant and very entertaining. Her big problem was that she was a dope dealer. This did not bother me as long as she left me alone. Well, we were all drunk again as we fell into the house. Sophie and I went into the bedroom because I had to lie down and she was sort of carrying me. As she lay me on the bed, I grabbed her and kissed her on the cheek and told her I loved her. My intention was not to provoke a sexual response of any kind, but sure as shit, it did. Her face swept around until our mouths touched and the next thing you know we were

French kissing. This kiss lasted at least a minute. It really seemed much longer. Then I just pushed her away and pretended to pass out. I had chills up and down my spine. She was a good kisser. I started beating myself mentally over the head about how I let it happen. I started wondering whether I was gay or not. Naturally, I knew I was not. So therefore, I must be a pervert. I honestly felt that Sophie felt the same as me. We never mentioned the kiss again.

Birt invited me back the following evening, alone, for a solo birthday celebration. When I arrived she was stoned out of her mind. She was very mellow and smiley-faced. She offered me a hit of acid (LSD). I did not want to appear to be a prude, so I accepted her generous birthday gift. She said it would make me happy and see things more clearly. As I sat there waiting, nothing happened. I did not feel happy or sad, I did not reach enlightenment of any kind, I just got upset. I wondered why everyone raved about LSD. After we spent some time together, I started to head for home. Birt quizzed me on if I was OK to drive or not. I assured her that I was. This was a foolish mistake. As I drove down Sauk Trail the houses started splitting in half. I could not see anything but imaginary things like trees falling in front of the car on a road that appeared to be like a roller coaster. How I ever made it home alive or without killing someone, was beyond me. These hallucinations could not be controlled. I kept telling myself they were not real and to get a grip on things, but that did not help. When I pulled into the drive, I eased into the house, snuck into my bedroom and sat there wide-awake until the next morning. I saw fireworks going off, falling stars and moonbeams. It was not nearly as exciting as I had hoped it would be. Actually, I wanted to have some type of intellectual high, maybe discover the equation to time travel, a cure for cancer, a solution to world peace. No, not me. I just had visions of nonsensical aberrations.

Eleven

Wigs were in. Naturally, I had two of them. One was a blond pageboy, the other a red shag. Mother was still working downtown so there were times we took the train together. Many times we would be on the train and our heads were itching from the wigs. Yes, Mom had a wig too. She would be lying her head back and snoring on the way home from work, itching the top of her head. By the time we reached our stop, the wig was like a hat on her head.

One morning, Sophie and I got on the train, heading downtown. I had my blond pageboy on. I was so tired that I fell asleep. This was rare for me. I never slept anywhere but in my bed. My head was leaning back so far back off the seat to the back that my wig fell off into this really cute guy's lap. Immediately, I slumped down into my seat and begged Sophie to grab it. She was cackling so hard that I thought I was going to kill her. The guy that had my wig handed it to her and smiled. I snatched it up, put it back on my head, and slumped down in my seat. This was the day that I learned to pin my wig on my head to avoid any future embarrassments of this magnitude. Sophie got off at the Van Buren stop and I got off after her at the Randolph stop.

As I walked down the street, under Wacker drive, a pigeon shit on my head. I fucking could not believe it. First, losing my wig, then pigeon shit. This must have been an omen. I clocked in and sat down at my desk, then I got the word to get into Mrs. Ryan's office. Mrs. Ryan said, "Tori, I am concerned about your absenteeism. You have missed an average of one day a month."

I thought , shit! I knew it, wig, bird shit, now fired. I said, "Mrs. Ryan, I am really sorry. I have not been very happy here." Hell, there I go again, shooting off my big mouth.

"What do you mean?" she said.

"Well, all you have me doing is filing. I am bored to death. I realize that I have to start somewhere, but I think you could train anyone to file." I was being kind. I really felt that a monkey could do this job.

Mrs. Ryan, thought this over and then said, "Tori, you are probably right, this job is not for you." My heart sank, as she continued.

"I feel you would be happier in another position in this firm. How would you like to work in the service department?"

I could not believe it. This marvelous individual recognized that I was not a lost cause. I jumped up, ran over to her and kissed, her on the cheek. "Mrs. Ryan, you will not be disappointed in me. I will be here every day and do a good job for you!"

Mrs. Gunther was called upstairs and informed of my promotion. I grabbed my personal belongings and went to my new office. This was not a private office, but rows of desks with about 12 people and thirty-five sales and service men. Mrs. Gunther was my boss in the Service Department. Mrs. Ryan was head of this district office, so I was still working for her indirectly. Thank God. I really loved her. For her to have the innate sense to recognize the best in people was humbling. Well, I was happy. My day went from my wig falling off, to a bird shitting on my head, to a promotion. Yes, I even got a raise.

The experience of working downtown was one every girl should have to go through. People are so diverse in Chicago. You could meet a new guy every day if you wanted to. After being faced with Jack's impotence, I was a little apprehensive about getting involved with another man. My mind still wandered back to Ron. I had heard from Bern that Cecelia was pregnant and they were getting married. This news devastated me and threw me into my work. I left for work at 5:30 A.M.. and got home every evening at 6:00 P.M. I was still taking the Illinois Central.

When I got off of the train, Ron grabbed me from behind, swirled me around and kissed me hello. I was shaking as I looked into his eyes, knowing damn well that Cecelia was pregnant. Ron said, "My God I have missed you. Don't say anything just let me talk. I love you and have always loved you, but you are such a hard ass and won't budge. You threw me at her, testing me. Did you ever think that I was testing you?"

I could not believe this line of shit. He loved me all right. The sleaze-bag knocked her up and was here whining that he loved me. "Ron, please spare me your bullshit. No one held a gun to your head. You have been with her for over two years and now you want me to believe that you love me. Go to hell."

He had tears in his eyes, "I do love you! I always have loved you! Please don't do this to me. Let's run away. I can't marry her."

I could see the terror in his eyes, but I had learned a lot about people. He wasn't here for me. He was here for the idea of me, the past passion, the girl that was not pregnant, with no responsibilities; freedom! "Look Ron, you need to straighten up and go home. I am not going to get involved with you in any manner whatsoever. You need to grow up." By this time we had reached Buckingham fountain. I sat down on the concrete ledge and gave him the speech about it wasn't as bad as he thought. He must really love her or he would not have stayed with her this long, and that fatherhood would be wonderful. I said all this as tears streamed down my face. He kept trying to grab me, just to hold me. I knew I had to stay away. I got up and started running back toward my office, and yelled, "Congratulations!" never looking back. As I got to the office, I was so shaken that I had to leave. Mrs. Ryan understood. For some reason she sensed my grief. I felt like someone had stabbed me a hundred times and I was leaving my body. I was floating up in the air and looking down on this pile of shit.

Sophie and I went out that night and I got drunk. She chauffeured me around while I drank and threw up. "Come on Tori, you're going to have to forget that creep. Get on with your life."

"Yea, you're right. I am never going to mention his name from this minute on," I slurred. That night we buried Ron. As far as I was concerned, he died.

I really became obsessed with work, because I wanted to live on my own and be able to afford it. I had an apartment in the new buildings put up in town, paying rent of $400.00, which was nothing to sneeze at. I got a part-time job working for Dick Huffman, a local realtor. He handled HUD and VA property management. He was an overweight, manic depressive, genius. Dick and his wife worked the business night and day. I learned to love both of them dearly. Being the genius he was, he always put himself in the capacity of cupid, always trying to find me a husband, feeling that I needed to get married and have a family.

Dick approached me about meeting a guy named George Bradley. Dick was rolling his blue eyes at me and smiling, showing his dimples and blushing as he said, "Tori, there is this really nice guy I think you should marry."

I was typing a VA report and looked up laughing. "You have lost your mind. First of all, I am not looking to get married, second, there is no such thing as a nice guy."

Dick waltzed over to me. "Come on now, he really is nice. Probably the most eligible bachelor in town. All the girls in town would love to catch him. Just let me introduce you to him."

"Forget it, Dick!" I did not want to be fixed up.

Sauk Village was a small town. Everybody knew everybody else. All my efforts in declining Dick's kind invitation to find me a husband did not work. He dragged George over from the restaurant next door to meet me, on Saturday at lunch time. George was a handsome, rugged, Creek American Indian mixed with a little German. He had blue eyes, the same color as mine, with light sandy brown hair. He wore blue jeans and a short-sleeved shirt with the sleeves rolled up like you see in the James Dean posters. Now this was 1970 not the 50's, but he still struck a chord in me. George drove a black Cadillac convertible. I could not tell you the year, but it had something like wings holding the taillights in. Naturally, he asked me out and I went.

We had a boring time, because this man did not like to talk. He just sat there at the drive-in and watched the movie. He didn't even make a pass at me, which was unusual. He just dropped me off at my door, which was the next building over from his.

The next day, I borrowed George's car and went to Mom's house to do laundry. The neighbor that molested me wanted to know why his car was at our house. I told her I went out with him, and she had a fit. She whined "He is so cute, I would love to go out with him." I thought, "You slime bag, you'd go out with anyone." The thought of her getting near him made me nauseous. I have not mentioned her name, because it is not worth mentioning. Then for some reason, I decided this would be the man I would marry. It could have been this little conversation, or the fact that Ron and Cecelia had tied the knot.

This was the year of Kickapoo Creek, the rock concert in southern Illinois. Kate, Sophie and I decided to go. This was unusual because none of us could be considered hippies or druggies. We felt that the music would have to be great, so to put up with the rest, would be worth it. How dumb can three people be? The drive was about three hours to this farm on a creek called Kickapoo. As we drove in, I knew we made a terrible mistake. There were so many people that you could hardly hear the music. Most of the people were drugged out of this world. As we walked along, you could see couples engaged in "washing the dog." I might have gotten excited if I was stoned, but here I am with my sister and best friend and these people are just fucking out in the open. These bodies were not those of Greek gods or goddesses. So there was no real beauty in it. Probably the beauty was lost in seeing the look on their faces of being dazed. They were best described as Zombies fucking. This was not the event of a lifetime, it was a disaster. Sophie was so embarrassed that I thought she was going to die. Kate and I were just disgusted. We walked around for about an hour and then hopped in the car for a four hour ride home. We were silent the entire trip. We were overwhelmed with a sadness that our peers had regressed to a scene from the fall of the Roman Empire.

Twelve

My mother was now having a stroke over George. I was seeing him on a regular basis. I had decided that I needed to be married, I was the right age, nineteen going on twenty. George was twenty-nine, going on thirty. The age difference did not bother me, but it sure bothered Mother. We became officially engaged in March. The ring George picked out was a pear diamond, about three-quarters of a karat. It was beautiful. No date was set, but George was thinking a year would be time enough.

Around the second week in June, we decided to marry right away. This was because we could not keep our hands off of each other. Since I was still working both jobs and George had a good position, we could afford to plan our wedding in three weeks. Mother also helped financially. She resented my marrying so young, before Kate or Joe, especially someone ten years older. She could not talk me out of it though.

We had a traditional ceremony, planned with a reception at the restaurant next door to Dick's. All the important people in town were invited and we had two people stand up. Naturally, Sophie was one and the other a girl, Jean, from Bowes, Inc. The best man was George's best friend, Buck, who lived with him on and off, and another guy that worked with him.

We were all at the church. I was in the back room with the girls, my mother and George's mother, when I started crying. Mother jumped up, "Tori, you do not have to do this. Come on and let's get out of here." Naturally, I really wanted to run out the door and never look back. This was not really what I wanted. All I could think of is nothing is forever.

Before I could get a word out of my mouth, George's mother piped up, "You can't just leave. There are people waiting for this wedding, and what about George?"

My mother answered, "To hell with them and George, let's go."

I was still sobbing so uncontrollably that it was hard to get the words out of my mouth. "I am going to do this," I stammered.

I just could not walk out and leave George stranded. George was such a good, kind, loving person. I did not want to marry him, because I knew we had nothing in common. I also did not want to hurt him. He deserved much better. I kept telling myself that at the time, I was doing the right thing. Sophie came up and grabbed my arm, whispering, "Damn it Tori, you don't have to marry this guy. Let's just leave. I love you and will stand by whatever decision you make."

I looked at her and said, "I love you too, and hope you realize that I can't just leave George standing here." Sophie then gathered up her flowers and headed down the aisle. Shortly after, I walked out of the waiting room toward Dad, and went off on what was supposed to be a lifetime commitment.

As I walked down the aisle with my father, who now was a skid row bum, I continued sobbing. I wasn't really thinking about the wedding, but Dad. Poor Dad. How did this happen to him? He had become so bad that he even hallucinated about dancing flowers. He had to have hemorrhoid surgery, so he got off the sauce for a couple of weeks and he had to stay with me to recuperate. It was nice having him with me so that I could take care of him. It was kind of hard getting up the nerve to pack his rear end with gauze and tape it up, because he was my father. However, I preferred that to constantly picturing him lying up on Madison Street in Chicago, drunk out of his mind, bleeding to death.

Since he had left home, it had become a job for all of us kids to take care of him. We had to see that he got fed, housed, clothed and medically treated. Every day, I wondered when a call would come in that he had been killed in a knife fight in a bar, or had been murdered out in the street. For him to be here today was a miracle in itself. The only one not here was Joe. He was in Germany in the Army. Thank God he wasn't sent to Vietnam. I missed Joe. He sent me a telegram congratulating George and I on our marriage.

When I finally reached the altar, the minister leaned over. "Are you sure you are all right?" I nodded yes, and I cried through the entire service, realizing what a mistake I had made and yet going through with it. Anastasia was only ten years old at the time. She asked Mother, "Who is that dog howling?" Mother said, "Shut up Stacie, that's Tori crying." Then everyone started to laugh.

When we got to the reception, Sophie was waiting at the door for me. "How are you doing, Tori?"

"I should have never done this. I am such a damn idiot."

"Aw, come on Tori, you're just scared. You'll be fine. George is a great guy and I am sure he will make you very happy."

"I love you Sophie. Thanks for trying to make me feel better. You know, I am probably more upset about me being married and you being single. I am going to miss our time together."

"Tori! You have lost it if you think we can't still be best friends. I don't care if you are married. I am still going to spend time with you and I am sure George doesn't care either way. Now let's forget this shit and have a good time."

I was relieved that my being married didn't bother Sophie. We scampered off into the reception and partied till closing.

We went on our honeymoon to Alabama. Yes, Alabama. We went to Gulf Shores, Alabama, and stayed at the Holiday Inn. It was beautiful. The beach was pure white and empty. It was like being on a deserted island. We also headed to Florida. Some friends of ours lived in Ft. Meyers and had a hotel. I loved Joey and Liza. They were the perfect couple with two beautiful children. For some reason their son, Robert, and I bonded like soul mates. He followed me around questioning me about everything. Our conversations ran from fish to motor cycles. Robert was only about seven at the time. He had blonde hair, brown eyes with a keyhole pupil that made him unique. Basically, the honeymoon went well. I was glad to be able to spend time with someone that could carry on a conversation, even if he was only seven years old.

When we got home, we settled in George's apartment for a short time. I was still working at Bowes, Inc. and commuting downtown. I had become very close to Mrs. Ryan. One day, she was in her office crying. Mind you, Mrs. Ryan was made of steel. She never flinched or showed any type of emotion. I went in and closed the door and asked what was wrong.

"Well, Tori, I am leaving Bowes."

"Why?" I questioned. Mrs. Ryan started cleaning up her desk, turning her back to me.

"The home office feels that they need new, young blood in here."

If she was going, so was I. I quit right away. She was the greatest. I admired her class and her character. I was mesmerized by her talent to get the best out of people, and her ability to perceive other peoples' feelings.

Thirteen

Sophie really amazed me. She had fallen in love with horses. She now owned two and rode them every day. Because I was married, I only made it out horseback riding with her a few times. Once we decided to go bareback. Sophie had mastered horses, so it was no big deal to her. Well, I had a problem just getting on. I had to climb a fence and kind of jump on Mino's back. She was a Palomino. Well, I jumped about four times and finally made it. Then Mino took off like a bolt of lightning. I was pulling back on the bit and screaming, "Ho!" Finally, Mino just stopped dead in her tracks and threw me to the ground.

Sophie came riding up, laughing her ass off at me. "Do you remember the first time you took me riding?" I shook my head yes. "Come on Tori, just get back on and we'll try again." So I did.

"Giddy up! Come on giddy up!" I hollered. Mino just took off. Gradually I got her to stop slowly without throwing me. My inside thigh muscles were killing me from digging into her sides, but riding bareback was a treat. We must have ridden for hours after that. It was great. I gulped the fresh air in as it swept up my hair. My God, what freedom. As I watched Sophie gallop over the prairie, I felt so at peace.

Our next adventure was scuba diving. I really wanted to sky dive, but Sophie was afraid. We took our courses in physics and water. We had to do so many open water dives, and then a final dive before certification by our Padi Instructor. Sophie had a big rear end and I had those big tits, so we both required a lot of weights. Our first experience with the diving equipment was in a pool at a motel. No big deal, put on your flippers, tank, and goggles and you're off. Ha! Sophie's ass would bob up and I would be floating straight up because of my tits. We would add more weights, until finally, we could stay under.

Our first open water dive was eventful. I got on all my equipment and put extra weights on to make sure I would stay down. As I entered the quarry, I purged my mask, turned my O ring on and started breathing through my regulator. I was sinking fast and gasping, no air was coming out. What a stupid ass! I didn't test the regulator. I was now drowning. The weights kept pulling me down and I refused to unhook them, because they cost too much money. I started to get dizzy from lack of oxygen and I began flailing in the water. Somehow, I noticed a pair of legs hanging off a raft and I grabbed them. This big burly guy grabbed me and pulled me to shore. He made sure I was OK and I apologized for grabbing his legs.

This was a near death experience. Big deal. I just went and got a new regulator out of the pile and jumped back in swimming as fast as I could to catch up with the team. When Sophie and I finished, I told her what happened. She started screaming, "Damn it Tori, you could have been killed. We should quit this. You're such a damn maniac, you probably will get killed."

"Calm down, just calm down, I just made a mistake. It won't happen again, so just forget it."

"Tori, if there is one more problem, I am quitting."

"OK, I agree."

Finally, we had reached the day for certification. Sophie was all nervous. We went to a quarry in Wisconsin for our dive. We had to go thirty-five feet, ditch our equipment, put it back on under water, and then decompress as we came up. This meant slowly climbing up while inhaling and exhaling properly. If you move too quickly under water, you can contract the bends. The bends is when too many nitrogen bubbles form in body fluids when going from a higher pressure to lower pressure to quickly. The illness can range from joint aches and pains to coma and death. Well everyone had done their dive except for Sophie and me. Sophie was bawling like a baby screaming, "I can't do this, I really can't".

"Aw come on Sophie. Everyone did fine so will you. I'll go next and let you know if there is something to be afraid of. Just watch me." I got into the water and went down with the instructor. I ditched my mask and tank, put them back on, got the OK sign to go up and then I made the mistake of shooting up. As I started to climb fast, the instructor grabbed my feet and pulled me toward him and punched me in the chest. I let out a big gasp of air and then realized I had made the most dreadful mistake of not exhaling properly while climbing rapidly.

When we got to the top, the instructor screamed, "Do you know what you did wrong?"

"Yes, but please, please pass me. I swear I will never do that again." He passed me. I swam back to shore and screamed to Sophie, "It was a piece of cake! You will do just fine." Then everyone started screaming, "Go for it Sophie, Go!" She did it and did better than me, no mistakes at all; perfect. We all jumped up and down and clapped for her as she came out of the water, beaming from ear to ear.

George and I lived with mother for two years, saving our money for a house, helping her out with groceries, and paying rent. It was a mutual relationship. We all got along great. Mother grew to love George. We saved enough money to buy a new home. The house was a split-level in Sauk Village. It was a lovely home, that we furnished with modern deco. We both worked and made enough to make the payments and eat.

I played the good wifey. I cooked and cleaned like a pro. I became obsessed with perfection. These expectations of perfection were for me, not anyone else. I really did not expect anything out of George. Usually, everything he wanted he got. One day, he started dreaming about moving to Florida and buying a trailer park. His mother lived in Ft. Walton Beach and he wanted to move that way. We had just been in our home two years. Naturally, I went with the flow. We sold the house, borrowed $5,000.00 from my mother and I sent him on to put the money down on the trailer park. I stayed at the house to pack and was going to meet him there.

The night before I left, George called crying like a little kid, "I can't move here I hate it."

I could not believe this idiot. I responded with, "You better have a logical explanation for this flightiness or you're going to a shrink when I get down there!" and I hung up the phone. Sophie was waiting for me in the car when I stormed out of the house. I had conned her into going with me so I wouldn't have to drive myself. We drove seventeen hours straight without stopping. All the way down I ranted about how stupid I was to get married and Sophie kept trying to calm me down. She loved George. Hell, Sophie loved everyone. When I got there he just whined how he hated it and he did not want to live there, blah blah blah. This was when I finally gave up. In my mind this was the end of our marriage. I lost any respect I had for George, and at that moment I realized that I could not live anyone's dream but my own.

Since we were in Florida, we decided to visit Joey and Liza, have a three week vacation and then head home and look for new jobs. We had a great time. Joey and Liza had sold the motel and gotten into charter boats. They owned two, a small six passenger and a large sixty passenger. Joey took us deep-sea fishing. Sophie caught a ten pound cobia and I caught hammerhead shark. George just moped around. Sophie took a plane home and Liza and I headed for Disney World with the kids. Joey and George stayed home with the boats.

Robert was now eleven and becoming more and more handsome. He wanted to go on space mountain, so I went with him. He sat between my legs and I wrapped my arms around him, holding on for dear life. We had so much fun, it was like being a kid for the first time in my life. Robert held my hand and dragged me all over the place. Our bond remained intact from the first time I met him. I loved him more and more with each moment that I spent with him.

Robert asked, "So, are you going to stay with him?" I could not believe this kid.

"What do you mean?" I said.

"Well, you know, after wanting to move here and now he doesn't. Giving up the house and your jobs." This eleven year old was smarter than George.

"Look, Robert, I don't know what I am going to do, but don't you worry about me. I will be fine." I had no respect left for George. Here we were vacationing like the rich and famous, owing my Mother $5,000.00, no jobs, and an eight unit trailer park that looked like hillbilly haven.

When we got back to Joey and Liza's, George was trying to get on my good side following me around like a sick puppy. I relented, and we made passionate love. The entire time I felt like someone was watching me. The next day, Robert was very cool to me, almost like I had violated him in some way. That evening, again George and I were entwined in passion, and I got the same feeling. While doing it, I started looking around to see if I could see anyone looking in the windows or through the drapes. Sure as shit, a shadow was lurking in the bushes. This orgasm was very unique. I should say thrilling. I never said anything to George, Joey or Liza. I could relate to Robert's interest in what was going on in my bedroom. I could also relate to this perverse sense of curiosity.

Regardless, I loved him and would not embarrass him or betray him, ever. What was worse than his curiosity was my enthrallment with him watching. So, how could I betray him? Besides, it was the best sex I had in a long time.

George and I were now in the car heading home. We decided we would move back in with Mother, since we had spent all of our profits from the sale of our home. We also had to start earning some money. George decided to go into the remodeling business. I went looking for a new job.

Fourteen

It was not a good time for job hunting, especially if you wanted to work local and make any kind of money at all. I answered an ad in the local paper for a receptionist at a local golf course. I now knew I had reached an all time low. Spending my working hours at a public golf course and country club was rather depressing. As I went into the office a matronly woman with thick eye brows and a white powdered face, red lipstick, black hair and big brown eyes greeted me. She took me back to her office and set me down for a very informal interview. Her name was Remember. After discussing my qualifications, she explained the pay and vacation benefits. No hospitalization coverage came with the job. She showed me the reception area and walked me out the door, telling me that she would call if I got the job.

The next day, Remember called, "Tori, we would love for you to come on board." I hesitated and then said "I am not sure that I want to work at a golf course." As the conversation went on, she basically begged me to take the job, and I did. After hanging up, I started kicking myself in the ass, for relenting to Remember. I hated pretentious people. The country club set reminded me of the foyer gang in high school. I had been looking since November, it was now January, thinking to myself that maybe a golf course isn't all that bad.

When Remember hired me, I had not yet met the owner or any of the workers, other than the woman I was replacing. She was about sixty-two with jagged yellow teeth, cropped gray hair with blue eyes and bushy eyebrows. Her name was Ethel. I had to learn to call accounts for collection, type cards, file, write up party contracts, and answer the phones, within two weeks, since Ethel was leaving.

I was sitting at the front desk, when a tall, sandy-blonde, blue- eyed man came strolling through the doors. He was dressed to kill with his $500.00 suit and a million dollar smile.

"Well, looky har. Where did ya come from Honey?"

I could not believe my ears, that southern drawl was unbelievable. Almost put on.

"Sorry, I am not sure what you mean. Can I help you?"

༄

As he walked back around my desk into the coffee room, he said, "No Honey, I own this place. My name is Jimmie Gallager."

My face turned red as I jumped up, "Hi! I am Tori Bradley". He shook my hand and went on into his Office. I had heard rumors about this southern fire ball from all the rest of the crew. Everyone dreaded the day he was coming in. I heard rumors that he was the biggest drunk in town, and the most belligerent one to boot. It did not take long to learn the truth.

The next morning he came in the office bombed out of his mind, screaming: "Damn it! Remember, are you an idiot. You must be stupid. Get the hell outa har!"

Remember ran out crying and the next thing you know my intercom line rang. "Yes?"

"Would you come in here please?" I wasn't sure if I wanted to go in and kill the shit head or run for my life. I went in. "Would ya get me a cup of kafey, Honey? I like a lot of cream and suga." Like a good little peon I ran and got the coffee. "Thank ya."

I mumbled, "You're welcome," as I shut his door and went back to my desk.

Then he started on the phone. For the next four hours all you heard was "Looky har," "Fuck Ya then!" and "Ain't that right?" I was not sure if I should quit now or stay and protect Remember. She was really very nice. I understood why she took the abuse. He paid her well; twice what I made and she really didn't do much but take his abuse and do some bookkeeping. As time went on, I lost a lot of respect for Remember.

We had domestic ducks that we kept in a pond by the office. Every morning I would feed them and watch them dive for food. They really became my pets. A car company that was next door to us called me on the phone. The manager told me that the ducks were out on the main road in front of the dealership and they were afraid they were going to get killed. I became so upset, I wanted to go get the superintendent to get them. This infuriated Gallager. He came in screaming, "You've lost your damn mind! I am not paying my help $10.00 an hour to baby-sit those damn ducks. If they get killed it's their own damn fault."

Well, I thought I was going to die. I lost it. I started crying and screaming, "I can't believe you. Those poor ducks are going to get killed because of you, and if they do I am never going to forgive you for it!" I was sobbing so hard that I was gasping for air.

A few minutes later, Gallager came out of his office and was trying to be sweet, chuckling, "Look out the door. Your ducks are coming around the corner of the fence." Sure enough, there they were all four of them. Now I stopped crying but was still steaming over Gallager's lack of compassion. I turned my back on him and would not speak to him for the rest of the day.

As time went on, I became very fond of Gallager. I guess because he was a drunk I could relate even more than normal to his suffering. Most drunks are kind, loving people, until they get drunk. Then Medusa shows up.

Gallager would come in the office bombed out of his mind at 10:00 A.M., break open a bottle of Jack Daniels, and continue drinking through the day. Here he was, a handsome, intelligent, millionaire with a great family but one of the most miserable son of a bitches in the world. He would get so drunk that he would start crying and whining about how unhappy he was. He was always saying he had nothing to live for. When I thought about it, I had to laugh to keep from crying. Gallager was so much like Dad. He had the world by the tail but always figured out a way to hate life. Funny how drunks want everyone around to be unhappy with them.

It was a beautiful spring day when Gallager came into the office and yelled to Remember: "Get into my office. Louise wants to talk to you!" Remember just rolled her big eyes and went on into his office as he walked out. Louise was Gallager's wife. A beautiful woman that never had anything to do with the business, but followed Gallager's orders like a sick puppy. She quietly went in and before I knew it, Remember came running out crying her eyes out.

Louise came to my desk and told me to go in and write Remember's final check. I could not believe it. This woman had worked for them for ten years. She was always on time and putting up with Gallager's belligerent wise cracks about her weight, or work, or anything demeaning that he could come up with. I asked Louise if she was sure and she nodded yes. After Remember left, Gallager meandered back into the office and told Louise to go home. A few minutes later the com line rang and he hollered, "Tori, would you come in here?"

I ran in and said, "What do you want?"

He said, "Kid this is your responsibility now, I am sure you will do fine."

"Gallager, I don't know anything about bookkeeping or running a business. I am not sure I even want to know."

As he got up and headed for the door he shot back, "You'll learn."

The next day, Gallager was on a plane to Florida and I was stuck running a business that wasn't mine. I worked from 7:00 A.M. to 9:00 P.M., six and sometimes seven days a week.

Besides learning the petty office work of payroll, accounts receivables, payables and general ledgers, I learned how to put financial statements together, do deed modifications, trust agreements, real estate contracts, Corporate Resolutions and just about everything one needed to know about a business. I lost all time this year. I worked myself into a dark hole. I did this not because I was driven to be successful, but to get away from George.

Fifteen

I became bored with the country club and decided that I would go along with another of George's dreams. He thought we would get rich if we opened a game room in Sauk Village. I never thought we would get rich, but I did think it might be fun. We started to investigate the strip malls and found a little store front that would do for the arcade. We named it "Wizards." We leased our pinball games from an Italian who split the collections with us. He had the keys and would come every night and open the slots, count the money out and give us our half. Our landlord, Joe Scorcese, was also Italian. I was crazy about Joe. He was gorgeous, intelligent, rich, and the epitome of class. He was always positive and up beat and never had any thing negative to say about any person or thing. He loved his wife and idolized his kids.

Scorcese would always stop in and see me whenever he had the chance. I could tell he was crazy about me too. "Tori, I have never met anyone like you. It seems that you have so much going for you. What is it that you would like to do with your life?"

"Joe, I really am not sure, but I do know that I don't plan on spending my life in Sauk Village. There has to be more to life than this. I would love to be as successful as you, but I am not sure of how I can go about doing that."

"Tori, one day you will recognize opportunity when it knocks at your door, and I want you to know you can count on me to help if I can." I enjoyed Joe's visits. I realized that Joe was the type of man I should have married, because he could have made me happy. What he could have given me was common ground, not monetary happiness. If you live with someone that is on a downer the whole time, then you will become down. This was George, a perpetual depression. I felt sorry for George. He was never happy about anything. There was no passion in his life or if there was, you would never know it. He had no excitement about life, no convictions; never able to laugh or scream at the top of his lungs, or even be dogmatic sometimes.

Wizards was a losing proposition. Besides being a financial drain, it was physically draining. The income did not cover the bills, so it was a good thing we still lived with Mom. George just wanted to lie around and not go in, so I worked at the Country club days, and Wizards nights and weekends. I enjoyed meeting new kids. As time went by I made friends with a Japanese kid named Mike and a neighbor kid named Harry. Mike was handsome and bright with typical oriental features. Harry had black hair with blue eyes and was Polish. Both were intriguing. Mike was into body-building and Harry was a pyromaniac. He would come into Wizards and tell me how he loved to watch fire. The more that I got to know Harry, the more concerned I became about his well-being. His father beat him up daily and his mother coddled him. I guess the abuse, love, abuse cycle caused him to become what he was. Just about every time I worked, Mike and Harry were there. We would play biplanes and all the pin ball games. Occasionally, I would let one of them win.

    We kept our money box for Wizards at our house and carried it in when we opened. One night after being out at a family affair, we came home and found someone had robbed us. The money box was gone. The box had half our rent in it, two hundred, twenty-five dollars. This might not seem to be a lot of money to some people, but to George and I it was whether we paid the rent or not. I was livid. I started questioning Harry and Mike about who would do this and found out it was probably the kids that lived across the street from us. I was currently driving an old white Cadillac that was as big as a boat, a 1972 Sedan Deville. I got Harry and Mike in the car and went over to the perpetrator's house, had them grab him, and put him in the back seat. I drove around town screaming, "Listen to me, you little punk! If my money isn't back at my house by noon tomorrow, you won't be able to walk for the rest of your life! I am not going to let you get away with this." Then there was silence as I drove back toward their house. I stopped at the corner and Mike got out, letting the thief jump out and run home. The next day, my money was delivered to the house.

    That December, we closed Wizards. I was going to miss Scorcese' friendship.

Sixteen

I was back working with Huffman Realty in the evenings. Dick was the same adorable person. I was sitting at the front desk waiting for a call, when in came a guy that looked like a Greek God. Mr. Personality personified. J. D. Conti was his name. He smiled and said, "Hi Beautiful. What is your name?"

"Tori Bradley."

He peeked into Dick's office, "Hey, why didn't you tell me you hired the most beautiful girl in the world?"

Dick rolled his baby blues. "Leave her alone J. D. She is just getting over a divorce."

I had finally decided to get out. I wanted to live. George was just content to roll up in a ball and watch TV for the rest of his life. He needed someone like himself. We did not have the same energy levels. I bounced off the walls and he stuck to them. For some reason, I really didn't believe in the sanctity of marriage. I know this makes me sound like a heartless bitch. Damn it, I was suffocating and miserable.

J. D. made it a point to come in every time I worked and

entertain me. He graduated with an MBA from Northwestern and was a loan officer. He used the excuse that he was waiting for someone to come in and buy so he could take their loan application. We became great friends. This was the first time in my life that I could actually say I had a male friend. I was becoming more and more infatuated with him. He started coming by the office during the day, taking me to lunch and still hovered over me at night at Huffman's. J. D. was a lot like Joe Scorcese but he had a different attitude about money. He loved to be cheap. That didn't deter my infatuation with him.

As time went by, we started to wander away for trips to Chicago, for a lunch at the Como Inn. J. D. was Italian and loved Italian food. We would talk about everything from family matters to politics to friends. He was intellectually stimulating. Actually, we were falling in love. Finally, our friendship turned into a torrid love affair.

J. D.'s best friend was Bruno Pacini. From the moment that I met J. D., all he talked about was his best friend Bruno. He loved the guy. J. D. smiled or chuckled every time he mentioned Bruno's name. One time J. D. was telling me a story about them being at a strip club watching a beautiful girl that J. D. rated a ten. She had tassels on her tits and when she moved they both whirled in opposite directions. Bruno just sat there with no expression at all. Finally he leaned over to J. D., "Christ J. D. is this what you call beautiful?"

J. D. could not believe what he was hearing. He shot back, "Bruno, you can't really tell me you don't think that woman is beautiful."

"No, I really don't," he said flatly. J. D. was flabbergasted. When he was telling me this he said. "Wait till he meets you, he'll go nuts. I am sure he won't find one flaw."

This was interesting. First of all I considered myself to be provocative looking but not a ten. Second, it appeared that J. D. was competing with Bruno. I started to worry about just exactly what part of our relationship was discussed with Bruno. Finally, as I was setting at the front desk of Huffman's one evening, in came J. D. with the most handsome man I had ever met in my life, or seen in the movies. Bruno was about an inch taller than me with black eyes, dark brown hair and a beard. He was built like a wrestler, not too rugged but sexy.

J. D. announced, "Tori, I would like for you to meet Bruno. Bruno this is Tori."

I said, "I feel like I already know you."

"Same here, but J. D. did not explain just how beautiful you really are," Bruno said.

J. D. smirked, confident that he had picked a winner. They both took me out to lunch the next day. I was amazed at how much alike they were, except that Bruno had true passion and was talented. Bruno played the piano. He could entertain us for hours with stories of playing Rush Street and all the local universities.

I thought that Bruno would be a great boyfriend for Sophie. She and Jim had split up, so she was depressed. "Sophie, how about going out with J. D., Bruno, and me? We'll go play a round of golf."

"I don't know how to play golf." She was fidgeting. I hated it when she fidgeted.

"So what! I have never played either, so we can both learn together. Besides, you will immediately fall in love with Bruno."

"I am not interested in falling in love again. I hate men."

"Aw, come on. Please?"

"OK,"

Great, I thought. She needed to meet someone different.

As soon as Sophie met Bruno, she was nuts about him. I could tell. Her eyes started shooting sparks; she was flirting and profiling. He, on the other hand, was hard to read. We were out on the golf course and J. D. was trying to show me how to hit the ball.

"Keep your head down!" J. D. insisted.

"Damn it J. D., my head is down, my tits are in the way!"

He chuckled as Bruno came over, "Tori, you're not holding the club right. Put one thumb over the other and as your swing keep your eye on the ball." I chopped at it again and again, but Sophie did much better than me. She had a great drive and could putt better than J. D. or Bruno.

"For crying out loud, Sophie, where did you learn how to play golf?" asked Bruno.

"I've never played," she primped.

Now, I was getting pissed off at her. I don't know why I got pissed off at her. It wasn't her damn fault I was a lousy golfer. I guess I was jealous. The next time I was up, I just flung my clubs after I missed about ten swings off the tee. By the time we finished, my face was blood red and I was huffing and puffing. I shot a 225. That's a lot of swings. Bruno shot a 119, J. D. a 125, and damn Sophie shot a 125. Not bad for her first time out. We all had lunch and then called it a day.

It was apparent that Bruno was not remotely interested in dating Sophie. You know these things when the guy doesn't ask for your phone number. Bruno didn't ask for her number. Sophie sensed it also. "Tori, they are both so much alike, except Bruno is my favorite. He is in love with you. I'll never hear from him," she said matter-of-factly as we drove home. Deep down, I was relieved. I was intrigued by him.

We all went out to dinner just as friends, not as dates. J. D. and I both knew that Bruno wasn't interested in Sophie other than as a friend. During the dinner, we started to discuss financing, when J. D. blew it: "Tori, you're a pseudo intellectual!"

I could not believe my ears. He just said it out of the blue. No damn reason whatsoever. I think he was pissed off that Bruno was hogging the conversation. I was about ready to kill him, but before I could open my mouth, Bruno said, "Damn it J. D., what the fuck is wrong with you? She is smarter than you are. Why would you call her that?"

I can tolerate almost any insult but that was a low blow. It was becoming more apparent that J. D. was envious of my relationship with Bruno. He was becoming more and more aggravating daily, trying to piss me off.

"I was just kidding her." J. D. was weaseling out. "Geesus, can't you take a joke?" he questioned as he looked over at me.

"Fuck you!" I shot back. Sophie just sat there, afraid to stick her two cents in.

The rest of our evening was very quiet. When we dropped

Sophie and Bruno off, I started, "Listen to me you dick head. Don't you ever insult me again in front of anyone or you'll get the tongue lashing of your life and I will embarrass the shit out of you!"

"Calm down Tori. I don't know why I did that. Probably because you provoked me.

I didn't think it was that big of a deal." I just ignored him the rest of the way home. I resent it when someone insults my intelligence. Probably because I never got to go to college. Fucking J. D. should have known better. Really, it was kind of funny. Sophie and I were from what one would call the other side of the tracks. J. D. and Bruno had upper class families that had some money and could afford to send them to college. People usually hang with their classes. For someone from Sauk Village to hang out at country club was highly unusual.

Seventeen

Bruno talked me into getting my real estate broker's license so that I could work for him part-time, at his real estate firm. J. D. was not happy about the idea, but could not stop me. As time went on, I grew further apart from J. D. The last one-on-one conversation with him went like this: "Tori, can you go out for dinner tonight?"

"No, J. D., I think we had better not. I have to tell you something. I think I am in love with Bruno. It is not what you think, we have not been involved. But I really do think that I love him."

J. D. was silent for a moment, then he frankly said, "You know Tori you remind me of Messalina and you should have the same punishment she had." Then he hung up on me.

I was so upset that I was shaking. Messalina was Caesar's wife. The wife of Tiberius Claudius Drusus Nero Germanicus to be exact. She had her head chopped off for arranging a secret marriage to Gaius Silius, one of her many lovers. Just thinking about having my head whacked off made me grab my throat and hold onto it for a while. Although I had not slept with Bruno, I might as well have. J. D. had described our lovemaking all the way down to the screams to Bruno. If you constantly talk about your lover to your best friend, you're fueling the fire.

My apartment was a one bedroom with an eat-in kitchen. I furnished it with plants, Italian oil lamps, a flowered couch and a bed that George made for me when I moved out. The bed had a canopy with wood posters and a crushed velvet headboard. How ironic, George making me a bed. The country club was within walking distance of my apartment, which was great and three blocks from Bruno's real estate office. My days consisted of working the country club, and my evenings putting in up time at Bruno's office.

Even though Bruno was my best friend, he was crazy about me and vice versa. The more time I spent with him the more drawn I became to him. It is funny when you meet someone sexy. People that have this quality are like honeycombs with bees all over them. They are constantly pursued by someone they meet even when they have not expressed an interest. We were both alike in that respect. There was always someone chasing us. Bruno made it a point to chase me. I was trying to not get caught at this time in my life.

Our fun times were spent playing Pac Man at a local restaurant or driving around looking at properties. We frequented the best restaurants, because Bruno loved to eat. Our favorite was Kon Tiki Ports in Chicago. They had the best bread pudding in the world. I would be stuck at the office during lunch and Bruno would bring bread pudding to me from Kon Tiki's. He was always doing little things to win me over.

Eighteen

We were having diner at Mary D's. This was our favorite romantic hideaway. We would sit in the corner at our favorite booth and lose ourselves in conversation about one of Bruno's adventures playing Rush Street. He was an excellent pianist. He played at the Chicago Symphony when he was five years old. From the time he was eleven until sixteen, he would sneak into the black bars in Phoenix, Illinois, and learn jazz. Then he graduated to playing universities. Finally he was playing up and down Rush Street. Bruno even played as a studio musician at CBS. I was amazed at how he just stopped playing and went into real estate. Oh sure, one in a million guys become a star. However, there are many stars with no talent and a lot of regular guys that are multi-talented and never discovered. Bruno was one of those guys.

We headed home after dinner for our usual nightcap. I had one glass of wine and Bruno the same. Bruno was dressed to the nines in a black suit that drew attention toward his big, black, doe eyes. As I looked at him, I savored the moment. He was such a handsome fellow. I was madly in love with him and had been so since the day we had met. Tonight I would let him catch me.

I poured us another glass of Merlot and as we sipped it, we talked about the day's events. One thing everyone could always say about Bruno and me, we never lacked finding something to talk about. We were always conversing about business, current events, politics, and our personal lives. We could talk to each other night and day.

As we finished off our wine, Bruno had his arm around me and started to kiss me. What a kisser! All signals were go. Then we tore each other's clothes off and made love all night long. It was as if no one else had ever existed.

From that day forward, I could not get enough of him, nor him of me. We learned where each other's beauty marks were, each other's scars from nicking ourselves when we were kids, and our ticklish spots. We ate breakfast together, tried to sneak off for lunch with each other, and after work we stayed with each other until the next morning. We were never seen without the other. I was lovesick. If he had to go to a late meeting, I would get flu-like symptoms. Our obsession with each other was frightening, yet reassuring. If I had cramps he would wait on me. If he had a cold, I would baby him. I knew no matter what, I would love this man until the day I died. I also knew that I wanted to be the first to go when fate dealt the hand of death.

When we walked into the restaurants or bars that we frequented, people would stare at us. We would sit away from everyone and lose ourselves in each other. Most people were in awe of our relationship. I guess, because most people have never experienced this type of love. This type of love is obsessive, compulsive love. When Bruno belched, I laughed. I never laughed at anyone else doing it. In fact, I thought it to be rather repulsive. When I wore my torn, old, raggedy house coat and had my hair in curlers, he still loved looking at me. When we were naked together, our imperfections became perfections. He could be sitting on the toilet with me standing right next to him and we would be talking about how to set up some type of advertising campaign for my business. There was no gender between us, we were one. We were synonymous with each other.

One afternoon we decided to take a long weekend to go to Turkey Run State Park. We got a room in the lodge. Bruno and I loved to watch deer. We decided to take a hike and go across the extension bridge off into the wilderness area to see if we could locate any. We hiked for about two hours until it seemed like no human beings existed. The birds were chirping and the trees rustling with squirrels. We made love behind a large oak tree on a cliff overlooking a waterfall. Naturally, I got quite excited every time Bruno touched me. However, this experience was especially profound. It was pure and natural. It was the earth, the wind, the water, and the sky.

Anastasia decided to move in with me for a short time. Most nights Bruno would stay over, so the three of us nestled in my small, one bedroom apartment. Our evenings consisted of cooking something Italian and then piling up on the couch on top of each other. Anastasia loved Bruno and he loved her. They bonded like brother and sister. It was amazing how her face lit up when he came into the room.

"Bruno, move over!" she said while worming her way next to him.

"You can't fit in here. Sit on the floor," he teased.

"This is my sister's couch, so you sit on the floor."

"Aw, OK, come on, I'll move over," He playfully said.

In December, it snowed quite a bit and the temperatures had plummeted to below zero on many days. I grabbed a comforter and covered us all up, while we watched the snow flakes pile up on the ground.

"Would you look at them? They are as big as silver dollars." Stacie said.

"I hope we can get out of here in the morning." Bruno said.

I just sat there staring at the snow, while they jabbered back and forth. I was so content having them both next to me.

Nineteen

Bruno's house was three blocks away. We often had battles because of the passion between us. There is a great turbulence when two people are obsessed with each other. We had to fight in order to breathe. After we got into one of our fights, Bruno went home. I decided to call him up, about five minutes later. Our fights never lasted more than fifteen or twenty minutes. I got no answer. Then I called again. He said, "Hello."

"Hi, I am sorry that I screamed at you." He then asked, "Did you just call here?"

"Yes."

"I think I hit my head," he said. His voice had changed somewhat. He sounded like a wounded animal. "Are you OK Bruno?"

"I don't know," he said, and just hung up on me.

I ran out of the house, and drove to his house. He was running around in his underwear looking like a wild animal.

He said, "Did you just call me?"

"Yes, Bruno."

A few minutes later he questioned me, "Did you just call me?"

"Yes Bruno. I think I need to take you to the hospital. Get dressed."

He opened the door to make sure his Sportster was OK. As he did this, I grabbed him by the band on his underwear and told him, "You can't go out there."

He just looked at me, as I led him into get his clothes on. Then I got him in the car and he said, "Where are we going?"

"To the hospital, Bruno."

A few minutes later he said, "Where are we going?"

I said, "To the hospital!" in a huffy voice.

Then he repeated himself.

I said, "Shut up!" Well, this little scenario continued until I got to Urgent Care. The doctor came in and checked him over. She ordered an X-ray. Then she told us he had amnesia and would not be back to normal for a few weeks. I could not believe it. He sounded like a broken record, almost appearing to be faking it, but the doctor was very sympathetic toward him and not very pleased with my impatience with him. I took the baby home. I was on my own because Anastasia had moved down to Tennessee to stay with my Aunt Suzanne for a while.

Bruno and I were sleeping when the phone rang. Anastasia was crying hysterically and I tried to calm her down. "Please stop crying and tell me what has happened."

She blurted out, "Aunt Suzanne shot herself."

I sat up in bed. "Are you sure?" What a dumb thing to say. Are you sure? I wonder why people say such stupid stuff when someone dies.

Cattails for Sophie

Anastasia said, "You have to go over and tell Mother. She just went into the bedroom and blew her brains out."

"Geesus Stacie, wasn't anyone home?"

"Yes, Uncle Ernie was there. He was sitting in his rocking chair having a beer, and the gun went off. She was pronounced dead on arrival at the hospital", she sputtered out in between her howling.

All I could think of was the son of bitch killed her. He might not have pulled the trigger, but he might as well have. Aunt Suzanne had threatened suicide many times. This time she drank a fifth of Jack Daniels to give her the courage.

As Bruno and I drove toward Mother's house, I recalled the many times Aunt Suzanne rolled into town with one of her seven husbands. She was kind and loving. A touchy, lovey, kissy type of person that appeared to enjoy life. She loved to eat, drink and be merry. I don't know where she got up the nerve to blow her brains out. That takes a lot of nerve. It is the end of the party. It takes a lot of guts to end the party. Then I remembered her threats of several years back. I guess she figured she had won in the end.

We pulled into the driveway and Joe was there, screaming and howling, kicking the garage door in. I told him to get hold of himself, because he had to be strong for Mother. We went in, I knocked on her bedroom door and woke her up, then I broke the bad news to her. She started sobbing and pushing me away. She didn't howl like her kids, she just sobbed. She did not want anyone around.

I called Anastasia back and told her to get home. She had nothing to stay in Tennessee for. She needed to be home with her family. Aunt Suzanne donated her organs to science and the rest of her was cremated. I remember her always singing some country tune that depicted the life she led. The one that stayed on my mind was "I'm Not Lisa," by J. Colter. I believe it went like this: "I'm not Lisa. My name is Julie. Lisa left you years ago. My eyes are not blue."

Twenty

Bruno always was working on some big real estate deal. This time it was a condominium on Marathon Key. He could buy the condo for $50,000.00, which was really a good price. Before making his decision, he wanted to go stay there, so we embarked on a vacation to the Keys. We decided to take Sophie along with us.

Poor Sophie never did anything much except work, so Bruno and I thought this would be a treat for her. We flew into Miami then rented a car and drove down to the Keys. As we crossed the bridges from Key to Key, I became more and more disappointed. I could not see any sandy beaches, just coral.

We reached the building in about forty-five minutes. The outside was nice enough, painted white with palm trees and flowering camillia bushes. The foyer was elegant with a chandelier and social room. Sophie got the couch, Bruno and I, the bedroom. What is great about the Keys is that the water on both sides is accessible. Bruno had never been boating in the ocean. I told him I knew how to drive a boat, so we went out and rented one. Funny thing about renting a boat there, you didn't need any experience and you could take the boat Gulf side or Atlantic. The owner didn't care.

The three of us climbed in the boat and I maneuvered it out of the marina, heading out the Atlantic way. The waves had to have been three to four feet, because as we kept going, the boat tipped up on its rear and came crashing down at the bow. We would pass a fifty footer and the people would be waving us back in. Naturally, I would ignore it. Bruno was becoming more and more wary of my experience. Sophie was becoming more and more scared.

Finally, after we had gone about a mile out, I decided to turn us around and head back. As I would cut the wheel, the side would tip, almost capsizing us. Sophie laid down in the middle crying, "You're going to kill us!"

Bruno started yelling, "Damn it Tori, I thought you said you knew how to handle a boat!"

I was actually loosing my nerve, because of their lack of confidence, so I screamed, "Fuck it! If you think you can do any better you're welcome to it," as I let go of the wheel.

Bruno was astounded. He grabbed the wheel and his face became red with rage. Then it was his turn to try and turn us around. Well, Captain America tried and tried and finally got us back on track without us getting killed. I yelled, "Great job, Bruno!" while Sophie kept still in the middle, lying in a fetal position with her hands over her head. I felt this was a good experience for Sophie.

When we got back toward the condo, Sophie begged to be dropped off at the dock. Bruno was still driving the boat, and had no idea of how to stop. He asked me, "I don't suppose you know how to stop one of these things?" I just shook my head no, as we hit someone's boat. The guy came running toward his boat, cursing under his breath. Luckily, there was no damage. Sophie hopped out and that was it for her, no more boating. Bruno and I took off on our own.

We decided to go on the Gulf side this time. I laid in the boat basking in the sun as Bruno found a little hideaway with cypress trees growing off the edge of the banks. He then anchored the boat, under my direction. "Just throw out the anchor and drag it along until it grabs bottom," I ordered. He did so.

Bruno took his shirt off and whispered, "Let's make love." I was a little apprehensive, but not enough to decline this generous offer. We nervously took our clothes off and made love out in the open under the hot sun. Then we lay in the boat just holding each other soaking up God's beautiful creation, blue skies and sunshine.

For some reason I started to get uneasy, so I peaked over the edge of the boat and got a jolt. Our anchor had broken loose and we were heading for a coral reef. To my dismay, another boat had done the same and all that was left of it was shattered pieces. Bruno jumped up trying to get the boat started. Nothing. Then he looked at the engine and found the rope that held the anchor was entangled around the engine. He screamed, "Tori, jump out and untangle the rope!"

"The hell with that, you jump out." I screeched.

"I can't, I'll get blood poisoning from the coral."

"So, I won't? Just grab the rope and lets swing in around and over until we get it untangled," I said. We did and right before we were ready to hit the reef, we got the boat started and took off.

The next day, Sophie had no desire to go boating, so we decided to go to Key West, because of Hemingway. I have never been the tourist type or any type of sightseer. However, I was always the type to go with the flow so off we went. The drive was tedious, bridge after bridge, water and more water and still no beaches. We finally arrived at Key West. This was such a disappointment to me. The commercialization was offensive. Gay lovers smooching each other was nauseating to Bruno. Heteros don't play kissy-face and huggy-pie in public, so why would he want to watch gays doing it? Then to top it off, we sat down on a bench, up comes a dog and it starts to hump his leg. That was it; we were ready to go. We took the tour of Hemingway's haunts, ate, and headed back. What a disappointment. Hemingway was an OK writer, but honestly, "For Whom the Bell Tolls" bored the shit out of me.

As we rode home, I hoped Sophie enjoyed her trip with us. Since her and Jim split up, she refused to date. She didn't want to talk about it. She would just tell me to mind my own business, if I tried to fix her up. So I just steered away from that taboo subject.

Bruno had a Harley Davidson, which he loved. We would take rides out in the country every Sunday. One Sunday we got a flat tire and it was eighty-five degrees outside. I was dressed in full biker gear and sweating. We walked the bike for about an hour until I begged Bruno to stop. I just could not go on. He decided to ride the bike with the flat tire to the nearest gas station while I waited for him. I plopped down underneath a shade tree on the side of the road and watched traffic go by for about an hour. Bruno pulled up with a woman in a station wagon.

"Tori, come on, get in," he said. I did. To my surprise, Bruno introduced me to Kim, his first wife. I thought I was going to have a heart attack. She was really very pleasant to me. But, here I am all sweaty with no makeup, and she is all dolled up. I bet she thought he had picked the bottom of the barrel. I said, "It is very nice to meet you Kim, and thank you so much for your help."

"Don't mention it Tori. It was no trouble at all."

When we walked in the door, I thought I was going to kill Bruno. Naturally, he did not understand what all the fuss was about. "Bruno, look at how I look!"

"Tori, you are beautiful and you look great. You are blowing this way out of proportion. Besides, she was the only one home for me to get a hold of."

"I would rather have walked," I responded. He never ceased to amaze me. Even his ex-wife was at his beck and call.

Twenty One

Bruno had found a two flat in East Hazel Crest that he thought I should buy. I always listened to everything he told me, then rehashed it in my mind and basically made my own decision. I looked at the building and fell in love with it. This was my first home that I bought on my own.

I was unpacking my dishes and cleaning up the first night when all of a sudden a rat crawled out of the fireplace and sat on the mantel. I shut my eyes and opened them again, looking the rat in its eyes. There it was, and it wasn't moving. I was scared shitless. I ran in the kitchen and grabbed a butcher knife, then ran into my bedroom and crawled onto the top of the bed. This rat ran down the length of the living room, up the side wall of the bedroom to the corner of my bed, and plopped its ass down and looked at me. It had big pink ears, black fur and a long, slinky pink tail. I started crying and screaming. The rat got scared and ran out of the room.

I got on the phone to Bruno, screaming hysterically, "There's a fucking rat in this house. You sold me a house with a rat in it!" Wham! I banged the phone down. Well, Bruno did not run over to catch the rat. He was such a chicken. Now, here I was stuck living with a rat.

Sophie came over to spend the night with me. Out came the rat. Sophie was being very stoic. "He's a rather cute rat. I think he is someone's pet. Maybe we should catch him and take him to a pet store or zoo or something."

I started shaking. "Listen, Sophie, I am not going to catch a damn rat and do anything with him. There have to be limits on what we have as pets. My limit is a damn rat."

I had not seen Bern since I worked downtown, so I was really looking forward to her visit. Her mother had called me all upset about the new love in her life, Sheila. Yes, Bern was now gay. It is funny how she dated several men and actually fell in love with them, and then decided she was gay. Her new love was previously married and even had a child. So, I guess you can turn gay. Sometimes men can be so brutal that women swear them off for the rest of their lives, I guess.

Well, Bruno could not believe it. He was so excited about two gays coming over that he called all his friends and invited them over. I was lucky that they all declined. I planned carry out so that we could enjoy each other. When Bern got there, I was amazed at her display of affection for Sheila. I mean she would blow kisses and Sheila would pat her hand and say, "You're great babe," every time Bern would get a correct answer in Trivial Pursuit. We played Trivial Pursuit and Bruno was elated that we were kicking their asses. When Sheila wanted more wine, after drinking a gallon already, she banged her glass down on the table and hollered, "More wine".

Bruno would jump up and run in the kitchen and get the wine. He would then get on the phone to one of his friends whispering about the evening's events, saying, "You need to get over here. I've never seen anything like it." Then he would hang up and run and pour Sheila more wine. She was sloshed by this time. I think Bruno was more entertaining than Sheila. He even called Anastasia and begged her to come over. I was in shock. I could not believe how open Bern was about being gay. I also could not believe how she took the verbal abuse that Sheila started doling out. The drunker Sheila got, the more abusive she became. If Bern got an answer wrong during the game, Sheila would call her a stupid bitch. I could not wait for the evening to end. It hurt me to see what had become of my friend from high school. The gay part wasn't the problem. The relationship was the corker. I wanted to actually beat the shit out of Sheila. However, I knew that Bern had picked this partner, so I had to keep my mouth shut.

As soon as they left, I called Sophie. "Holy shit Sophie, you would have never have believed it in a million years. They were actually a couple!"

"Did you like her?" Sophie was being serious.

"What the hell do you mean, did I like her?"

"Well she is Bern's mate, so did you like her?"

"No. I didn't like her. She is abusive toward Bern. I guess if she wasn't so abusive I would have liked her."

"Maybe she was just drunk."

"For chrissake Sophie, who gives a fuck why she was abusive, she just was abusive."

"Well, Tori, Bern made her choice. What would you say if she didn't like Bruno?"

"That is not the same thing."

"In her eyes it is."

It fucking infuriated me when Sophie was right.

Twenty Two

Bruno and I spent most of our weekends at Dad's playing cards with him and Kate. Poor Kate. She was Dad's partner every time we played. She and Dad were always accusing Bruno and me of cheating. We played Rook. Dad would get so pissed off, he would throw his cards on the table telling Kate, "They are giving each other some kind of signals." We loved these card games. Dad had finally quit drinking and smoking. Not of his own volition, but because he was very ill with emphysema. He would make chili and Bruno would eat half the pot. Anastasia lived in the same building as Dad. She would run by and grab something to eat and shoot the bull for a while, then scamper off to go out with her friends.

I enjoyed sitting back and watching Bruno and Dad banter back and forth like two roosters. I had become close to Kate and looked forward to our time together. She was always such a lady. I often wondered why she tried to please Dad so much. It was as if she was seeking his love out and never quite grasped that it was given. Dad really loved everyone.

"Damn it Bruno, you have to be giving her signals!" Dad shouted.

"No sir, not me. We are just lucky. Tori and I are two lucky ducks."

"Bullshit!" Dad shot back.

For Bruno's birthday I gave him a Harley Davidson Wide Glide. It was black with a gold, custom paint job and all kinds of chrome. We would get on the bike and ride out in the countryside every chance we got. The Wide Glide was much more comfortable than the Sportster. One day we went on a poker run that took us into Merrilleville, Indiana. On a poker run you stop at different places designated and pick up a card. Whoever got the best hand won a trophy. We were doing quite well, my hand was close to being a straight. All of a sudden the wind started blowing about fifty miles an hour. Dirt was whirling around and it started to rain pellets as big as quarters. Since sissies wore helmets, naturally Bruno nor I had one on. I wiped mud from his glasses as we kept riding down Route 30.

The wind was so strong that we were riding sideways on the bike to the point that I could have touched the ground. I started screaming, "Bruno stop the bike and pull over or we're going to get killed!" He kept going. "Bruno, stop the bike!" On he went. "Bruno, stop this damn bike!"

He turned around and hollered, "Jump off!"

I was flabbergasted. As I choked back the tears of anger, I kept wiping his glasses so that he could see. I realized he was scared to death. The lightning was becoming more and more violent and the sky was black. Finally, he pulled over to the side of the road and told me to get under this large oak tree that was on the edge of this country home. I looked at him like he was nuts and said, "Have you lost your mind? It's lightning out here, we'll get killed!" We both had jeans and Harley T-shirts on. Our faces were covered in mud and we looked like two drowned rats. We stood facing the farmhouse shaking from the chill of being wet, when the door opened and a sweet little lady asked us in. She gave us towels to dry off with and told us a tornado was in the area. A few minutes later it had blown over and we left, thanking her profusely. I was surprised that this lady was so kind. We really looked like a couple that belonged to a motorcycle gang. We finished our last stop and got back to the meet and I won a trophy for my poker hand. It was then that I wondered if I had a brain full of beans or liked living on the edge.

Bruno loved biking every weekend. Most of our free time was on the bike. One Sunday morning we took the bike downtown to Rush street in Chicago. We stopped at La Marguerite for lunch. We wore our usual jeans and Harley T-shirts. As we walked out the door, three guys looked at my tits and said, "Sure would like to suck on those."

I was shocked. I wiggled by them and said, "Bruno, did you hear them?"

"No. What did they say to you?" I told him and he got so upset that I thought he was going to kill someone.

He started running for his bike with me chasing him. No sooner did I get my leg over the back bar than he took off. He was riding down Rush Street on the wrong side of the road, speeding head on to the guy's car that insulted me. We were almost nose to nose with the car when Bruno swerved to his right and kicked their car door. He pulled over to the side of the road, jumped off the bike, and started screaming, "Call the cops. That guy hit me." He was holding his leg up in the air, rocking back in forth like he was in pain.

The police came and Bruno sent them after the guy. I leaned over and whispered, "If you don't get your ass back on that bike and take me home I am never going to speak to you again."

"I can't, I think my ankle is broke," he whined.

I shot back, "I don't care if both your legs are broke. Take me home."

He hobbled on the bike and we drove in silence all the way home. His bike had a toe heal shift, which put a lot of pressure on his ankle. No sooner had I gotten him home than I had to take him to the emergency room. Yes the shithead broke his ankle. Naturally he was hurt, but I am the one that suffered six weeks. I had to wait on the crippled, crybaby, hand and foot as penance for opening my big mouth.

This was the year of the motorcycle. Sophie had to have one, so she went out and got a little Honda. Her eyes beamed with joy at the accomplishments of getting the bike and being able to ride it. I was at home watching TV when she called me up crying saying she had fallen off the bike and thought she broke her arm. I ran over to her apartment and took her to the emergency room. The doctor said she broken both of them.

As I drove her home, I asked, "Damn it Sophie, how'd you break both arms?"

"I was turning into the complex and hit some gravel. I

kinda went blind in my left eye. As I came down, I jumped and fell on my arms instead of falling with the bike on me."

"Damn it Sophie, did you just use the front brake?"

"I don't think so. I swear I hit the gravel and the back of the bike just slid out from under me."

"Look Sophie, you have to promise me that you'll get rid of the bike or else I am going to be a nervous wreck every time I think about it. You could have been killed."

"Don't worry Tori, I'll get rid of it." For the next six weeks, I got up at 4:30 each morning and went over to Sophie's and helped dress and feed her. Her mother took the evening shift. I wasn't sure about who suffered the most.

Bruno and I went to a house in Calumet City to look at some Chihuahuas that were for sale. I was going to get one for Sophie's birthday. They looked like miniature deer. The breeder kept them in a closet with papers all around. Bruno fell in love with the runt, so we took her. We wrapped her up and carried her over to Sophie's place. This dog was as small as the palm of my hand and was attacked by Sophie's Doberman, so she had to go back to the closet.

"Tori, I love her, but Brutus will kill her. Why don't you take her home?"

"No way, Sophie. I'll just take her back. The breeders said I could bring her back if Brutus didn't take to her."

"She is so cute. I don't know how you're going to take her back and just forget that you ever seen her."

Sophie was right. As Bruno and I started driving, he said, "Tori, I am not taking this dog back to those people for them to lock her in a closet."

"I know you want this dog, so just say you want the dog."

"No, I just don't want this dog abused."

"Hell, Bruno, the dog is not abused. They have to keep them somewhere. Just say you want to keep the dog." He would not say it. Secretly, I had fallen in love with the dog too.

Baby Dumpling went everywhere with me. I took her to my office in my purse. She would sit on her blanket and sleep. Then she would chase customers out the door or beg for food from all the employees. At night, she would crawl in between Bruno and me and risk being smothered to death. One night, I had to leave her at home. When I finally got there, she ran around in circles, howling. I picked her up and told her I loved her and she just howled. From that day forward, I would whisper in her ear, "I Love You," and she would start howling. I was crazy about that damn dog.

Twenty Three

Dad became very ill with emphysema and was given just days to live, so Kate, Joe, Anastasia and I were spending night and day at the hospital. One day he would be coherent and the next delirious. His doctor was always trying to get us to go home, because he felt our presence there was prolonging Dad's life. Well, that was all we needed to know. That is when we moved into the hospital vowing not to leave day or night. One of us was there constantly. Finally, the hospital sent Dad home to die. Since I had a home close to my office, we decided to put a hospital bed in the living room. Kate took days and I took evenings and nights. I slept at the foot of his bed on the couch and if he needed anything he could just ask.

I had to get up each morning and bathe him, change his catheter, wipe his ass, feed him, and wait for Kate. We would both change his bed and get him settled for the day. I went to work and came home to feed him dinner and get him settled in for the evening. This went on for two months. Far longer than the five days the doctors gave him. I thought I was going to die when Dad started bleeding from his penis and I had to remove and clean his catheter and clean up all the blood. I thought he was going to die right then and there. I kept thinking, there is no fucking dignity in death, none, zip.

Kate was a professor and had to go back to school. We now had the dilemma of what to do with him in the day. We had heard about a VA nursing home that was recently built in Manteno, Illinois. So, Kate and I checked into it and found it to be nice and clean, because it was new. We made plans that when she went back to school, we would put Dad in the nursing home. I was devastated over having to do this, but there were no alternatives for us. Before making this move, Dad just wanted to smell the fresh air outside, so Bruno and Joe carried him onto my back porch and tied him in a chair. The sight of this was so heartwrenching that we all just bawled and bawled. Dad, no matter how sick he was, never complained about his pain. Now, he might bitch about his toenails not being cut right or I forgot to clean his ears, or his food was too hot, but never about not being able to get out of bed or not being able to breathe.

The day came to take Dad to the nursing home. I cried hysterically as Bruno, Kate and I followed in the car. After we got him settled in his room, Kate and I went snooping around to see if we would be going to war over improper treatment of any kind. It was amazing, the difference in this home and the old Chicago VA Homes. It was beautiful. The personnel were kind and appeared to be good care givers. Dad had his own room near the nurse's station with two cute nurses that treated him like a king.

Cattails for Sophie

I visited the nursing home every day after work. This went on for a year. During this time I forgot about everyone else in my life, including Bruno. One day, I left the nursing home early and went by Bruno's house, only to find some girl's bra in the couch. When he came home, I started screaming, throwing and punching. I basically tried to kill the poor bastard. Then I left. All I could think of was how could my soul mate sleep with other women.

Now that Bruno was out of my life I started bar-hopping with Sophie and Anastasia. The age difference between Stacie and me was nine years, but I could relate to my little sister in many ways. Kate and I were only four years apart and never got into any fist fights or petty arguments. On the other hand, Anastasia and I could have killed each other during many of our battles of the siblings. Afterward, we would both run around for a day or two like wounded animals, and somehow one or the other would call each other up to ask something or another, never mentioning the fight.

One night we went out and were sitting at the bar having our usual one drink. In our younger days we could drink gallons. Then we changed. After watching our alcoholic father come off skid row, get seriously ill and have to again become acquainted with the family, we never drank more than one drink. Sophie didn't drink too much either. Maybe a half a glass of wine.

Sophie started to get dizzy and told Anastasia and me that she was going to the bathroom. Anastasia and I waited for about ten minutes. Finally we both headed for the john. There Sophie was, neat as you please, laying passed out on the floor. "Damn it Sophie, wake up!" I screamed. I was scared. Sophie wobbled to her feet. "Are you OK?" Anastasia questioned. "Yes. I just felt like the blood drained to my feet and the next thing you know, I was coming to." We helped her to the car and headed for home. Bruno was following us. I just forgot about Sophie and started worrying about Bruno.

When I got to the house, he just drove by. I decided to get back in the car and go for a ride. Next thing you know, he was behind me at a stop sign. He jumped out of the car, pulled the car door open and said, "Please Tori. Take me back, I love you."

I could not contain myself. I wanted to kill him. I jumped out of the car and started punching him in the chest and slapping his face like a psychopath. I was crying, yelling, punching. "Get the fuck away from me! You are nothing but a dirty rotten scoundrel! A rogue! A rattlesnake! An insecure piece of shit! A user! A dick head! A dirty rotten motherfucker!" I jumped in the car and sped home.

Every night and during every day, he drove by the house. He sat across the street from the house and watched who came and went. He would call. I would hang up. I was so miserable, not because of him following me, but because I missed him. I honestly can say I felt he was my other half, my true one and only soul mate. Our inseams were even the same. Finally, after two weeks of this, I told him that I would talk to him.

We met each other for dinner at our favorite restaurant, Mary D's. The first thing out of his mouth was, "I love you, Tori. Please, I beg you please don't just throw our love away. I can't live without you. I can't function."

I thought the same thing, as I shot back with, "When you love someone you don't go out and screw someone else."

"I know," he said, "I don't know why I did it."

"Bruno, you better figure out why you did it and with whom. I won't even consider taking you back without those answers."

"Tori, I love you. I can't live without you. We were meant to get old together. Please won't you just forgive me and forget this ever happened?"

"No Bruno, not until you tell me why and with whom and then I will think about it." I figure I was crazy for wanting to know who but why was very important.

Finally, Bruno said, "All I can tell you was that my ego made me do it. You haven't been around because of your dad. I know that is horrible to say, but Geesus Tori, I guess my ego just got the better of my judgment and me. It was Rosie."

I thought I was going to choke on my salad. He fucked Rosie Rotten-Crotch. This bitch was his friend's girlfriend who fucked everyone they both knew and then some. "Geesus Christ, Bruno, Rosie Rotten-Crotch? You slept with Rosie Rotten-Crotch? How in the hell could you? What about Morgan? Does he know?"

"No, Tori, I didn't tell him. He is getting rid of her anyway. She seduced me I didn't seduce her."

We finished our dinner in silence and I told him that I would think everything over and get back to him. As he walked to his car, he looked like a whipped puppy. I understood his affair. It is hard to ignore the pursuits of others, especially when your partner is ignoring you for months on end. For Bruno to even come clean and say it was nothing but his ego, showed he still had some character. I could not believe he did it with Rosie. We had even gone away weekends with her and Morgan. I thought we had some semblance of a friendship. I called her up the next day and read her the riot act. She just hung up on me. What was she supposed to say, "I'm a whore?"

I let Bruno beg and beg, knowing damn well I would take him back. I had sworn I would never take someone back that cheated on me, but here I was taking Bruno back. I could really and truly understand this indiscretion. I didn't like it, but I understood it.

When Christmas came, Bruno was acting like a proud peacock. I knew something was up, but I just went on about my business as if nothing was happening. Then he gave me a beautiful marquise diamond. He didn't ask me to marry him. He just gave me the ring and assumed that I would. I told him he shouldn't have, and stuck it in my jewelry box, never putting it on my finger. By taking this action, he knew I was not even considering marriage. I would have died for Bruno before the Rosie Rotten-Crotch episode, but now it was time for him to serve penance.

Twenty Four

I was sitting at Bruno's office trying to do some bookkeeping for him when my mother called from my office and said, "Tori, the hospital called and your dad is dead."

"What?", I screamed.

"Your Dad is dead."

I started screaming at the top of my lungs, "Dad is dead. He can't be dead. Bruno said he was OK last night."

Anastasia was there and she was trying to calm me down but I was absolutely hysterical. I got Bruno on his car phone, screaming hysterically, "Damn it Bruno, you said Dad was OK. He is dead! You lied to me!" Then I hung up without waiting for him to respond. I ran out the door and went home. I had moved in with Bruno in August. The house was a three-story contemporary cedar home with vaulted ceilings and a winding staircase that was difficult to maneuver. I started running throughout the house from floor to floor screaming, "Dad is dead! Dad is dead!"

How could this be? I had spent every day going to the hospital over the past week and was too tired to make it last night, but Bruno went for me. When he came home he told me that Dad wanted to know where I was and he wouldn't even look at him, and he was just being stubborn. I pictured Dad lying at the hospital, gasping for breath and screaming for me and I wasn't even there. My God what a bunch of shit. Dad is dead. Dad is dead. What am I going to do? He kept crying out over the past few months that he wanted to live. He wanted to live. Even though he could not breathe and the nursing home had to put him in the hospital because of respiratory failure, he wanted to live. All I had heard out of his mouth for months was, "I want to live. I want to live. I want to live!"

It finally dawned on me. Besides the fact that Dad wanted to live, I was never, ever, going to see him again. A cold chill came over me and I started screaming, "Dad is dead! Dad is dead! Poor Dad! Dad is dead." I just kept running to each floor of the house, crying, screaming, howling like some dog that had been hit by a car.

Bruno came running into the house and was crying, "My God Tori, I am so sorry. But I swear he was fine when I saw him." I just kept running and howling. I called my friend, Lonnie Spago, and told him to go get Dad. Lonnie was a good friend that owned a couple of North side Funeral Homes. A lot of the production companies shot movies out of his places. Kate, Joe and I wanted to see Dad before he was cremated. Anastasia refused to go. We all were dead set against cremation, but Dad's last wishes were fulfilled. He wanted to be cremated with a brief memorial service if his kids wanted

Cattails for Sophie

one, and then to be taken back to West Virginia and buried next to his mother at the family cemetery.

The service was at a local Chapel. Mother even came. We all took turns saying something or doing something. We sang the hymns he loved. "Are your garments spotless? Are they white as snow? Are they washed in the blood of the Lamb?" rang throughout the building. I read his favorite poem, "Footprints." Dad swore to us he wrote Footprints for one of his AA meetings, but we didn't really believe him. He was delirious when that statement was made.

After the service, Kate and her husband drove Dad to his final resting place, the top of a mountain in Beckley, West Virginia. On the way home from the service, I remembered what this little, old, black lady friend of mine told me: "Tori, don't you be sittin there death watchen, cause as soon as you turn your back, he'll just slip away." Dad always wanted us around. He didn't want to die alone, but I guess we all really do die alone.

When Kate got back, we could hardly look at each other. One afternoon, I don't know how we got on the subject, but she mentioned that Dad had told her husband that he wasn't sure if Kate was his kid or not. "Kate, was he drunk when he talked to John?" I asked.

"Probably," she said.

"For crying out loud Kate, you look just like him. He probably said that because he was drunk out of his mind and trying to get John to feel sorry for him. What else did he tell John?"

"He intimated that Mother had been around the block when he had met her."

"Damn it Kate, he was the one that went around the block. And so what if she did go around the block, you still are the spitting image of him and you know how he lied when he was drunk! Hell, don't you remember him calling us up and telling us about flowers dancing outside his window?" I finally realized why she always was seeking his approval. How stupid she was not to see that she looked just like Grandma and Aunt Verna. Hell, she took more after his side of the family than Mother's. All of us kids did.

After this little talk, Kate and I kind of drifted apart. We no longer had Dad to take care of. Our baby was gone. I went to work every day, loosing myself in the business, and went home every evening and looked out the large wall of windows into the field of cattails. I kept daydreaming about going out, picking one and lying in the grass, lighting it up and pretending to smoke it. Then when I came back to reality, I would just cry like a damn baby.

Twenty Five

I had not been spending a lot of time with Sophie because of Dad. I could not face anyone. It was just too hard. Her mother called me all upset one day. "Tori, Sophie is in the hospital."

"What is wrong with her, Mrs. Eaton?"

"We are not sure, they are running all kinds of tests. We're hoping she's just allergic to something." Sophie was loosing sight in one eye, having seizures, and losing muscle control. Allergic reaction, my ass, I thought.

Sophie was in one hospital right after another over a thirty day period. Finally, the Mayo Clinic diagnosed her with Multiple Sclerosis. Then, I remembered the accident on the motorcycle. She said she went blind in one eye. Also, her passing out in the bar. Damn it, I should have paid more attention to her.

What bothered me the most about Sophie being so sick was the life she had. She never married, never had her own apartment and never really was as lucky as me. Now here she was dying. Why in the hell do you suppose God decided that

Sophie has to die and I didn't? I guess that was one of those Moo questions. You know, the answer is Moo when there is no answer. Well Moo shit, or is it Mu?

During one of her episodes, Sophie was rushed to St. James Hospital in Chicago Heights and was in intensive care, delirious. Bruno and I drove over to see her. When we showed up, her mother was relieved to see us. We told her that we would sit with Sophie and to take a break with Mr. Eaton and have some dinner. Sophie was in an oxygen tent. She had pneumonia, but it was getting better. As I sat in the room with Sophie, I rubbed her feet and patted her forehead, hoping this might give her some comfort. Sophie started whispering, "Tori come here."

"Sophie, did you say something?" I said, as I leaned over her bed.

"Tori, do you remember what we promised each other when we were kids? You know, our pact we made when Puff died?" she said with a raspy voice.

"Yes Sophie, I remember." I said as my mind went wild thinking Geesus Christ, Sophie wants me to kill her.

She then went on, "Tori, just get me something. Anything. Sleeping pills or whatever. Don't you see I can't put my parents through this any longer. Tori, my dad has to bathe me, feed me, and change my under pants. For crying out loud, Tori! Help me!"

I leaned over to her, "Sophie, I love you, but what we promised when we were kids was one thing. They might find a cure for MS and you could become well."

She just turned her head away from me as a tear rolled

down her cheek. Honestly and truly this pitch I gave her was a line of bull. I wanted to help her. I would have wanted her to help me if I was in her shoes. The fact was, I was afraid of the ramifications. I was chicken poop. Then her mother came in all cheery and stuff.

I wanted to know if this hospital felt she had MS. Apparently, to diagnose MS, you had to go through a series of MRI's. If lesions are found on the spinal cord or brain, chances are you have it. It was also possible that Sophie had contracted Encephalitis. Her horse had it, and she had to put him to sleep last year. Medicine is nothing but a Sherlock Holmes mystery, a game of intrigue and deduction. I began wondering if Sophie got MS from being around her horses. Someone else who I knew had it, also rode horses. On our way home that evening, I cried for Sophie almost as if I was at her funeral. Bruno kept trying to console me, but I just sobbed and sobbed.

The next morning, I thought again about Sophie's request and what I would want her to do for me, if I were in her shoes. I got some halciom and valiums together and wrapped them in a Kleenex. I put them in my pocket and slowly walked to the car, almost feeling like I was going to an execution. I was in a daze. I just drove to the hospital and went right into Sophie's room without even getting a pass. She was looking better and was smiling. "I knew you'd come through for me. I just knew it. Tori, I am dying anyway. I just can't keep mom and dad torn up this way. You don't realize how hard it is to take care of me."

I started bawling as I eased over to her bed and slid the

Kleenex under the covers into her hand. "I love you Sophie, and I know you would do this for me, but promise me that you won't take these today and you will think about this tonight before doing this."

"I promise."

We couldn't talk anymore; we just bawled our eyes out. I was howling and choking at the same time. I left the hospital the same way I went in, dazed. As I drove home, all I kept telling myself was that I did the right thing. No one knew but Sophie and me. It was now her decision.

Twenty Six

As Bruno and I drove over the bridge, it was almost like a dream. We could not believe that we had done it. We had just closed on a condominium on Hutchison Island in Jensen Beach, Florida. The condo had two swimming pools with a jacuzzi. We had our own pier. One side of the building overlooked the Indian River, the other side the Atlantic Ocean.

Bruno was squirming around in the driver's seat, more excited than any kid I had seen at Disney World. His eyes beamed with sheer delight at the million dollar view we were now privy to. We decorated as inexpensively as possible. As we ran around from shop to shop, I would say, "I'll take it."

Bruno would say, "How much?" It was funny, I never thought about what I spent. I always knew I had the ability to work and pay for whatever I wanted. This deal was an exception. We took everything we owned and borrowed against it so that we could pay cash for the condo. One hundred fifty-five thousand smackers is a lot of money for a second home, especially when you are not wealthy. One thing about it, between my real estate investments and job, I had squirreled away a tidy sum. Bruno, on the other hand, was highly leveraged in all of his businesses.

We had peach tile and carpeting installed. The furniture was pure Floridian, a blonde, oak dining room set, couches that were peach and green with a tinge of blue, and a tall wooden egret that you could crank his head sideways, with long bronze legs. I loved that damn bird. I even talked to the stupid thing every time I moved his head. I always felt that everything had soul. This egret had a ton of Soul. In less than one week the entire place was furnished so that we could be comfortable when visiting.

At night we would cuddle and make love with the sliding glass doors open, listening to the beat of the waves crashing against the beach. During the day we would walk the beach, hunt for sand dollars, swim, get in the jacuzzi, make love, take a nap, and eat. My absolute favorite time was watching Bruno play solitaire on the patio, while I listened to Mozart's piano sonatas. I would find myself crying while listening to Vladimir Horowitz play Mozart's concerto KV 281. It never ceased to amaze me how God created such talent and never gave me any of it. His dark side always intrigued me. I felt as if I was dragged into the underworld while listening to his requiem. Each time it played, I thought about Sophie.

My third passion after Bruno and Mozart was hunting for sand dollars. Poor Bruno would be scouring the ocean floor for sand dollars with me for about two hours every day, unless we found one right away. I fell in love with those little sea urchins when I read the "Legend of the Sand Dollar." You can see the Easter Lily on one side with a five pointed star in the middle, representative of the Star of Bethlehem. The poinsettia is on the other side. The holes equal the four nail holes and the spear wound make up the wounds at the points of crucifixion. When you break one, on the inside are five little miniature doves of peace.

You know God must have made them. Otherwise, who put all those important symbols on them. The great big boom sure didn't. The way I see it is with the big boom theory, how the hell did all those symbols get on one tiny sea urchin? Plato would say the artist painted them on in his mind and when he put it on canvas, it became so. God sure did paint a beautiful picture. When I would find one, I would look it over again and again, mesmerized by the beauty and precision of such a creation.

Bruno and I loved to drive the area looking for manatees. One day we happened upon the power plant in Ft. Pierce. We pulled into a marina that was known for manatee sightings. I got on my hands and knees and leaned over the edge, screaming back to Bruno, "Hold my feet so I don't fall in." He was nervous about me hanging over the edge of the pier, but went ahead and grabbed my feet. I splashed the water and up popped two manatees. They rolled over on their backs and I rubbed their bellies. It was so beautiful. These beautiful sea animals have big, beautiful, brownish-gray eyes and the face of an elephant that had its nose amputated. They would roll over, I would splash the water, then I would pat their bellies over and over again. Bruno, looked on in awe. "Come on Bruno, climb down here and pet one."

"No thanks Tori, I don't want to pet one. I am enjoying watching you pet one."

As we got up, I noticed a man cleaning his fish. A little, tiny white egret was standing on the deck. He would cut some and then throw the bird a piece. It caught it without a flutter. All of a sudden this huge pelican was hovering over and coming in for a landing. As it landed, we noticed it had one leg. As he swooped down, he leaned over on his left wing and scooted with his right leg, almost rolling over. "Bruno, please go give that man some money for a fish so we can feed the poor thing. He is probably starved to death."

Bruno just watched for a minute, then he said, "Tori, that pelican is well fed. Look at him. He must get sympathy everywhere he goes." Before I could turn around, a great big fish was thrown at our one-legged friend, then another. He gulped them down and then took off.

We would sit on the pier for hours, watching the pelicans glide by as the salt air brushed our cheeks. The waves turned into white caps and then rippled into the shore. The ocean is so vast. I kept thinking about Sophie, wondering if she would take the plunge. She had been cheated and I was so blessed.

Twenty Seven

Sophie Eaton died. She was rushed to Mercy Hospital and pronounced dead at 5:30 P.M. Christ! I was hysterical. She did it. My God, she did it. No, I did it. Damn it, I murdered her. I know I didn't shove the pills down her throat. But damn it, I sure did give them to her. Shit! I should have never taken them to her. I was so sick that my stomach felt like it was rolling over every two seconds.

Bruno could not calm me down. All I did was run through the house screaming, "Sophie is dead! My God, Sophie is dead!"

It was a repeat of the scene from Dad's death, only these howls were scaring Bruno. He could not understand my hysteria.

"Tori, get hold of yourself. You didn't want her to suffer. She was ready to give up. She told you herself that she was ready to go." After hearing this, I just screamed and sobbed some more. Bruno finally got in touch with Dr. Sarama. He prescribed valiums for me. I took one right after another, and still felt the pain.

Mother, Bruno and I went to the wake. It really is weird how people rally around at funerals. I wondered why they didn't all have get-togethers before death. All our old neighbors were there. Anastasia, Joe and Kate meandered in and paid their respects. Mom, Bruno and I stayed the evening. Mom tried to console Sophie's mom and dad and I tried to console her sister, Sue. How the hell do you make someone feel better when someone dies? It is even a bigger task, when you're the cause of their death.

I don't know who I felt the sorriest for, Sophie's parents or her sister. Sophie's parents had taken care of her while she laid in the bed. Sue assisted on weekends. Her dad cooked for her, bathed her and entertained her during the day because her mother still worked. I hoped that he would not have a nervous breakdown, not just because Sophie was gone but because his baby died. Sophie's mom was another story. How do you tell someone that it will be OK after their child dies? Shit, Shit and double Shit. That is what I thought about this. Shit, Shit and double Shit.

The funeral home was packed. It was like old home week. Everyone you haven't seen in years crawls out of the woodwork. As I sat there and watched everyone coming in, I kept thinking that Sophie would be pleased. We all chatted about her and what a great person she was. Her mom and dad were pleased that everyone turned out. I said my good-bye silently. "So long my dear friend. You gave me strength when I needed it most. I experienced life because of you. I love you Sophie and I always will." It is really kind of funny how people start to look back on their lives when someone dies. There is no future, just the past.

Cattails for Sophie

I could hardly stand it when the funeral director asked us to leave. He wanted to close the casket for the night. I thought this was going to kill Mr. and Mrs. Eaton. Instead, they tried to console me. If only they knew the truth.

The next day Sophie was buried near some trees. She loved birds and trees, so her parents picked a grave out at a cemetery in Homewood, Illinois, called Washington Memory Gardens. Sophie implored them not to use a local funeral home or cemetery, and to make sure she was waked by someone she did not know. She also did not want an autopsy performed. These wishes were followed through with, in spite of the fact that the doctors never could honestly say that it was MS. They had found one lesion on the brain stem. It never changed. They never found any other ones. I was relieved that there was no autopsy. I ordered a limousine for Sophie's parents because I wanted them to ride behind the hearse in style. No matter how you look at it, funerals are for the living.

When they lowered her into the ground, I could hear the lowering device squeak. Each time the lever turned, a squeak. I had picked some cattails from Plum Creek, where we found that box nosed turtle. I waited until everyone had walked back to their cars then went over to the opening, peering over into the vast hole with the casket top shimmering from a beam of sunlight. I stood there, slowly dropping the cattails one by one. That's all I remember.

Twenty Eight

I had built Gallager's business to a point where he was making over two hundred and fifty thousand dollars a year. He began to resent me. His Atila started to show. He would come in drunk or drinking and make snide remarks. Then he started to try to sell the business behind my back. It was unfortunate, but no sale was permitted without my approval. So Gallager had to wait until my management agreement ended or pay me five hundred thousand dollars, neither of which he wanted to do. Any perspective buyer also wanted to negotiate my employment for five years. This was impossible for Gallager to do. Also, his greed was insurmountable. No offer was ever close to what he wanted.

Finally, he came up with the solution to both of our problems. He wanted me to buy the place. I, on the other hand, was happy doing what I was doing and felt he should have been just as happy. One morning he came in, plopped his ass down in a chair in my office, and started to order me around. "You should buy me out, since I can't sell this until the agreement ends. You should buy me out." I just ignored him and this just provoked him more. "Damn it Tori, you better give me some respect here!"

I finally had enough, "Get the fuck out of here, Gallager. My agreement says that you can't come in the office. So get out of here!"

His face grew red and he started screaming, "I am going to knock your teeth down your throat!"

"Go ahead. You just go ahead. I dare you to hit me. I will kill you if you touch one hair on my head, motherfucker!"

Then my entourage of employees came in. Carol and Mary were black and beautiful. They put their hands on their hips, tilted their heads back, and Carol said, "Gallager, I think you had better leave now."

I honestly thought Jimmie felt he was going to be jumped by the three of us. Out he ran, straight to Bruno's office. "Bruno, ya know what that woman has done to me? She has threatened to kill me. Now that ain't right," he claimed.

Bruno said, "Jimmie, what did you do to her? You know that temper of hers. You had to have done something."

"Naw, I just told her she should buy the business. Ya know Bruno, it would be good for her to buy that business. Hell, she has run it for almost twenty years," he said in a much calmer voice.

"Will you finance her?" Bruno asked.

"I would have to think about it," he said as he walked out. Jimmie was obsessed with getting rid of me. We were at one time the best of friends.

Over the next three months, Bruno was the liaison between Gallager and me. Gallager set the price, while I was trying to

Cattails for Sophie

set the terms. We did not speak to each other at all. Poor Bruno got it from both of us. I felt the price of two million five hundred thousand dollars was out of line, since Gallager owed me the five hundred thousand on my contract. Gallager thought I was stealing the place. Finally, the deal was made. I was to pay his price and I could dictate the terms. Two hundred thousand dollars down, a ten year amortization, with a five year balloon at 10% interest. It was funny, but I never flinched when I agreed to this. I had no idea of where I was going to get the down payment. I had about forty thousand in cash and that was it, the rest of my money was tied up in real estate. Bruno never worried about it. He always knew I would come up with the money somehow. I only had sixty days. I borrowed against my cars, Jensen Beach, and borrowed the rest from my mother. I got my two hundred thousand dollars together one week before the scheduled closing. It was funny, somehow Bruno had more faith in me than I had.

I was sitting at the lawyer's office. Gallager was across the table from me with Bruno to my right. Attorney Cohen was next to Gallager. He represented Gallager and I represented myself. I was closing a multimillion dollar transaction. My hand was shaking and I was crying. Each document I signed would bring out another howl of tears and whining. Mr. Cohen leaned over and asked, "Tori, are you OK?"

"Yes. I am OK." Then I would whimper and sign another page.

Bruno whispered, "This will make you a millionaire. Don't worry honey you are doing the right thing." It took less than twenty minutes. It was over. I had done it.

I looked out of our window at the cattails and smiled. It was as if I was running from this thing my entire life. Driving myself farther and farther, for what? I was never motivated by money. I was just driven. Driven in work, driven in play, driven in sex. Somehow, because of this drive, I got lucky. But no matter how much I accomplished, I stayed depressed. I knew that if Sophie had made it to the other side alive and well, she would have contacted me. Nope, she was dead and gone. Never to be heard from again. Dead is dead.

I had been sick, so finally I made an appointment to go to the Doctor. A chest X-ray discovered black spots on my lungs. The nurse told me that I needed an immediate cat scan to see if I had cancer or emphysema. When I went home and told Bruno, we both just ran away from each other and cried. I could hear him crying downstairs and I laid in the bed howling. I was crying for him and he was crying for me. I tried to howl softly. Bruno, on the other hand, had just whimpered. What would happen to him without me, his best friend. This went on for two days. Those doe eyes of his were red and swollen. I thought my heart was breaking.

As I laid there on the table while this tube scanned my lungs, I kept praying to God for a reprieve. I got one. Apparently, I had scar tissue on my lungs from smoking. I was relieved, but somehow disappointed. I kept thinking about Sophie, dead, in that cold grave, by herself without me.

There was no way that anyone would have thought Bruno and I could have gotten any closer than before. When I got

Cattails for Sophie

tired, he got tired. When I was sick, he was sick. Our love grew deeper than ever before. We would hold hands as if we would never be able to hold hands again. We would make love as if we were saying good-bye. The only thing I had ever hid from him was the pills that I gave Sophie.

Twenty Nine

Bruno had fallen in love with a quaint little town called Lemont. Lemont has rolling hills with a church on every street, or so it seems. The downtown district is old store fronts that have been turned into antique shops or restaurants. The people are all American, good Joes if you know what I mean.

This one particular subdivision called Egrets Landings is a gated community on Egrets Golf Course. Every weekend, Bruno would get me in the car and drive me to Egrets Landings to look at these lots on the back side of Blue Heron Drive. I fell in love immediately with the beautiful setting of a lagoon and the golf course behind it. Great Blue Herons with Great White Egrets were fishing in the lagoon. Clusters of Canadian Geese swooped down to fish. On 51 Blue Heron Drive sat this French-style brick farmhouse that had been for sale for quite some time. The house was never lived in and was built for a couple that had to back out of the deal due to some unforeseen circumstances. The next door neighbor's house was an English Tudor.

Our other neighbors were skunks, Mama, Papa and three babies. We named them the Le Pew's, after Richard Bunkow's Looney Tunes character, Pepe Le Pew. Every night about 8:30 P.M. they crawled out of their burrow and walked in a line across the street to the adjacent country club. Mr. and Mrs. Le Pew were training their babies to find food, and all the other necessities in life. The Le Pews were out every night showing their young how to find food and shelter. This is pretty ironic, since a lot of our kids are just thrown out in the streets to fend for themselves.

When we entered the house, I didn't take an immediate shine to it, probably because the kitchen cabinets were knotty pine. I kept saying, "Look at these ugly knotty pine cabinets. This builder must have been out of his mind."

Bruno nodded in agreement, "Maybe they will replace them with whatever you want if we buy the place." I looked out the kitchen window and saw the lagoon and cattails. It was 51 Blue Heron Drive, 51 was the year of my birth, and there were cattails. That was it for me, "Lets go make an offer."

Bruno swung around, "Tori, are you sure? Maybe we should look around some more."

"No, this is where you want to be. So let's do it." Two weeks later, we closed the deal.

I put recliners with tapestry upholstering and a stripped blue couch in the Great Room. An oak wall unit housed a large horse on its hind legs that almost touched the twenty foot ceiling. Baby Dumpling's bed was tapestry to match the decor. I also had a brass bed for her. That damn dog was still

Cattails for Sophie

such a joy. We trained her to go on under pads. Every time she would go potty, she would come out of the bathroom slinging her head toward there for us to go see. Then we would all clap and give her a bone. I now called her Thumper. I don't know why I called her Thumper, but she knew both her names. That dog was pretty darn smart. I would scratch her head and she would take her paw and try to grab my fingers to make me continue when I stopped. I would tell her, "Say I Love You," and she would immediately start howling.

The coffee table and end table were designers that were leather, styled in book forms with gold pages. The titles engraved on the bookends were Jack London's Sea Wolf and Plato's Republic. I found these tables about two weeks after I finished rereading The Republic. Naturally, this omen meant that I had to have them. They also had a lot of soul.

While sitting in the Great Room, I could see into almost every room on the lower level. Bruno's private room housed his computer and keyboard. Sunday mornings, Bruno would go into his room and play his keyboard. To please me, he would play Mozart's Sonatas as if I were attending a private concert. I would shut my eyes and dream of being with him at a concert of Mozart's in Salzburg in 1784. We were dressed in eighteenth century formal wear. Bruno was the dashing gentleman that paraded me around on his arm.

Still, every time I started to enjoy something, Sophie would pop up in my head. I kept reminding myself that I did what was asked of me.

Thirty

I had not seen Sophie's parents since her funeral. I just couldn't stand to be in the same room with them. Mother asked me to stop and see them, because they had been hashing and rehashing the idea of having her disinterred and autopsied. Apparently, they were concerned about not knowing what really caused her death.

As I walked up the driveway to their door, I got cramps in my stomach. The last thing I wanted them to do was order an autopsy. Naturally, I was concerned about them finding the overdose of drugs in her system.

"Hi, Mrs. Eaton, how are you?"

"Oh Tori, it is so good to see you. I am fine, come on in."

As I walked in the house, I began sweating. It almost seemed like I had started to run a 102 degree fever. I looked over at Mr. Eaton, leaning over the kitchen table smoking a cigarette.

"Hi, Mr. Eaton, how are you?"

"Fine, Tori. It is good to finally see you. I know how hard it is for you to come here."

"No, Mr. Eaton, it is really good to see you. I just thought it would be hard on you and Mrs. Eaton to see me."

Mrs. Eaton was getting out some cookies and making a pot of coffee. The house looked the same. All Sophie's pictures were still all over the house. I tried desperately to control myself when I saw our graduation picture standing on the TV cabinet.

"Tori, you know we are considering having Sophie's body taken up and an autopsy done. Now, I know everyone thinks it is horrible, but the Mayo Clinic said probable MS. They never confirmed anything. We made a terrible mistake by following through with her wishes anyway. What if she had something that Sue could get that was hereditary?" Mrs. Eaton said as she poured the coffee.

My hands were shaking and sweating. I could not look her in the face. I just kept scanning the room. She was busy gathering up some cookies she had made to put on a tray for us to eat. Mr. Eaton was taking out little, white paper plates and napkins and neatly laying them out for us.

"Mrs. Eaton, you should do what you feel is best for you and your family. Sophie would understand." I was not about to try to dissuade her. I had made up my mind that if it was going to be so, then it would be so.

"Oh Tori, I am so glad you are behind us on this otherwise there would be no way I could do this. She loved you more than anything in this world."

"I know Mrs. Eaton. I felt the same about her." I said as tears swelled up in my eyes.

Every day since Sophie died, I thought about her. Not just

about me giving her the pills, but about her. I missed her. I loved her. I would never forget her. I was becoming so sick, I thought I was going to puke. I talked with Mr. and Mrs. Eaton for an hour and I can't really tell you what was said. All I know was I knew that my fate was sealed. Had Sophie known what trouble I was in, she would have never asked me to fulfill our childhood promise.

Thirty One

I had just gotten home from the doctor's office when the phone rang.

"Tori, this is Dr. Sarama. We need to do some further tests. Your hemoglobin count is high and we need to find out why."

Immediately, I thought the worst. All that ran through my mind was that I had the big C. Surely, I thought, it has spread so my prognosis is shit. I just laid down and kept imagining being terminally ill. All I could think of was being entombed in a crypt without Bruno next to me, all alone. How in the hell am I going to die alone without Bruno? I thought. Funny thing, I used to worry about how I was going to live if something ever happened to Bruno.

When he came in, I gave him the news. He just broke down and cried. He could not stop crying. He would not look at me, he just cried and cried and cried. I had never seen Bruno cry like this. I laid still in the bed and listened to him whimper. This went on for hours into the night. Finally, he came to bed worn down from his pain, and grabbed hold of me. We clung together until morning.

I always thought that if something like this ever happened, I would be a martyr and take it with my chin up. The hell with martyrdom, I was scared out of my wits. I was also being so selfish, wanting Bruno close to me at the time of my demise. How could I consider wanting this? I wanted him in the crypt next to me. I never knew one could be obsessed with another even in death. This life obsession with Bruno was different, but to want him in the crypt next to me was mortifying.

We had to attend Uncle Joe's funeral at Infant Jesus Catholic Church. As I sat there, I began to cry hysterically. All I could think about was this will be me soon. Then, it dawned on me. I had no church affiliation, so who was going to preach at my funeral? Where would my services be held?

I said, "Bruno, just promise me one thing. Promise me you'll be buried next to me even if it is fifty years from now."

He was crying, "I promise."

Now, I thought to myself, I was one selfish bitch. How could I do this to him? I should be a martyr, a fucking martyr. I couldn't help myself. I loved this man. I loved the hair in his ears, his bald spot, his round belly. I even loved his lapse in memory. I would never ever see this wonderful man again or feel his butt in my belly when we slept. I would never hold his hand while walking the beach. I would never be able to watch him devour the spaghetti that I made for him. All I could think of was the stupid stuff. I began worrying about him having to watch my deterioration. I worried about him wiping my ass, swabbing my dry mouth, watching me go bald, and listening to my gasping for air. I could not suffer through his suffering. The best thing about this would be that I would finally pay for Sophie's death.

I went into the doctor's office prepared for my death sentence. The damn table was one of those old metal things that are cold. It kind of reminded me of a morgue table. I don't know why, because I had never seen a morgue table. In walked Dr. Sarama. "Hi Tori, how are your feeling?"

"I feel terrible. I feel like I am fading."

"Well, you're not fading. You just have a little blood disorder called polycythemia. Yours is the type that is caused from the medicine you were on. So, we are just going to take you off of it and you will start feeling better."

"Thanks Doc," I said as I jumped down from the table.

All I could think of was running and telling Bruno about my reprieve. I wondered why I had imagined the worst. Maybe I thought I deserved to die. Well, it doesn't really matter. Bruno was elated. Deep down, no matter how damn guilty I felt about Sophie, I was relieved that I had not been given the death sentence.

Thirty Two

I had learned to push Sophie to the back of my mind, except when I looked out the window at the cattails. I looked at them everyday at least five times. So, it went from 100 times a day to five times, or maybe ten times.

Every time I thought about what I had done since she died and how she had been cheated out of her life. What a lousy hand she was dealt. Then I would cry and think about all I had and what I had accomplished, and tell her I wished she was here so she could enjoy life with me. I thought it was time for me to go visit her grave.

As I drove through the gates, I could not believe it. A beautiful white statue of a young lady with a fountain pouring blue water over her, overlooked the area that Sophie was buried in. Little white and black ducks were diving in the water for algae. A mallard was sitting in a duck house that was painted blue with maroon windows. I felt so at peace. Then a chill came over me as I heard the bells ringing throughout the grounds. I knew, then, that Sophie was home. This was the place to be. As I walked to her grave, which was in front of three giant granite crosses, across the road from the pond, two squirrels were chasing each other. She would have loved them. I walked right to her grave. It was funny. It seemed like it was the first time I had ever really seen the place. Yet, I walked right to her grave.

I sat down next to her headstone and starting cleaning around the vase, getting ready to place the cattails I had brought with me. "Damn it, Sophie, I miss you. It just isn't fair. I miss you so much. I know how hard it was for you to have you dad wiping your ass, so don't think I am mad at you. I could never be mad at you. Hell, I don't even know what I am talking about. Sophie, I feel so guilty. It seems like if it wasn't for me, you would still be here. Fuck, Sophie, why don't you give me some kind of sign. Just a little sign to let me know you are OK." I cut the cattails small enough to fit in the vase and arranged them so that they kind of laid on the edge of the vase opening. Then I just sat there trying not to even breathe so that I could hear the birds sing. Then I looked over at the pond and watched the water bead up and roll off the ducks' feathers as they dunked their heads in and out of the water. "This place is beautiful Sophie. I am glad your mom and dad put you here." All of a sudden a little squirrel scampered over toward me. It ran up to me and sat right next to my hand. I had a cattail in it just rolling it up and down my fingers. The squirrel grabbed the cattail and ran off, almost as fast as it came. Chills ran up and down my spine. I smiled and looked up into the heavens, "Thank you God." When I got in the car and headed home, I felt at peace.

There was a knock at the door, which was very unusual. No one can get in the gates without the gatekeeper phoning us to get permission. Bruno went to the door, and I overheard someone say, "I have a warrant for the arrest of Tori Bradley."

"For what?' Bruno screamed.

"Murder."

I started shaking and getting cramps in my stomach. I became numb. Then I became relieved. It was over.

Bruno started pushing the officers out of our door, while I grabbed him and tried pulling him away. "Bruno, leave them alone. I have to go with them."

"What do you mean?" he yelled.

"Bruno, I gave Sophie pills." I whispered.

He just started crying. "My God, Tori. Didn't you think about what would happen? Didn't you care about us?"

"I love you, Bruno. I would have done the same for you."

The next thing you know, I was carted off to here. I know you are here to determine if I am a cold-blooded murderer. I am just a best friend. So, when you print the story, don't paint me as someone evil. I did it because she asked. I did it because I loved her. I did it because of who I am.